Flowers For The Journey (A 4 Story Collection)

by

Jason Blacker

PUBLISHED BY:
Lemon Tree Publishing
Copyright © 2013
Jason Blacker

**Visit www.JasonBlacker.com on the web to stay
up to date**

Editing: Dragonfly Editing

ISBN: 9781927623282

Table of Contents

WHEN THERE WAS ONE   7

CAN YOU PLEASE BE QUIET   47

MY SON AND I   83

FOREVER FAMINE   119

ABOUT JASON BLACKER   167

When There Was One

"Geez, that's a good question. You want to know how it all started?"

The interviewer nodded his head. They were sitting in Kevan Mallon's apartment. It was a threadbare place that didn't contain much. Kevan was on a couch that looked like it had come from the Salvation Army decades ago. It was a dirty burgundy color and the fabric had been worn smooth. It was hard to see the paisley patterns it once showed with pride.

You couldn't be sure if the couch was dirty as part of its color or if it was dirty from lack of cleaning. On his lap sat a scrawny cat. She was a tabby with a torn left ear. Her back was arched as she stood on Kevan's thighs as he rubbed her along her spine.

The couch was small. Just a two seater really and Kevan sat on the left side of it. He sat in it deeply. Not because he was fat, people weren't fat anymore, but because the couch was old. The springs sagged like tired old men.

The right side of the couch was tucked up against the corner of two walls. On the right of Kevan sat a pile of old magazines. They were mostly time and Life. The top one was Life magazine. It was dated 16 November 2037. The title of it was Armageddon. The picture was of riots. They could have been anywhere, but they were in Toronto. That's where things had come unleashed.

The interviewer, his name is Autumn Blood, sits on a wooden chair. A spindle on the back rest is missing. You can count four of them instead of five. Autumn Blood, you'll understand that name in a bit, sits straight. If you look at him closely he seems to shimmer, like his skin, the color of ours, is mercurial. It seems liquid.

Autumn Blood doesn't blink for a long time. And when he does, he does it slowly, like he's savoring the moment. The curtains are drawn in here. But they're thin curtains made from a thin fabric.

They're the color of skin, almost as thin. The light comes in, and if you look closely you can see lots of flecks of dust in it.

When the light catches it right. These are our ancestors. These flecks are pieces of me and you. Of Kevan, of Smog his cat, but not of Autumn Blood. He doesn't really exist. Not in the sense that we do.

Smog jumps off Kevan's lap. She approaches Autumn Blood. Thinks better of it and then hisses at him. She's old and her mouth opens up showing only three teeth. Autumn Blood looks down at her and smiles. He reaches out and touches her. Scratches her around the ears. She likes that.

"Sorry," says Kevan, "she's not used to visitors. What did you say your name was again?"

Autumn Blood looks up at him. His eyes look weary. He seems tired, but he's not. Even though it's been a long journey. He's been here under two years. Humans have kept him busy, but he is not tired. He just looks that way. He blinks slowly. He can still see Kevan through his eyelids. Seeing is more than light. It is memory and photons. All these photons whizzing by like computer code. He watches them whizz through him, and Kevan. Like embers spat from a fire. Bright white little dots. Like rain, like torrential rain.

"Autumn Blood," he says, his eyes still closed.

"That's a weird name," says Kevan, "if you'll forgive me for saying as much. Especially for a reporter."

Photons are like harmless motes of dust. Like the motes of humanity that he swims through on this Earth as they call it. It's like swimming through a pond of scum. He doesn't mind it, but he can taste them. Even though he doesn't want to. They're sharp. Tangy, with the violent, acrid, metallic taste of blood. That should change in time. If he fulfills his destiny.

He remembers once. Seems like a long time ago. When there were no photons. When all he had was thick, syrupy, delicious nothingness. Blackness, some called it. But it was more than that. It was a cradle of divine emptiness. He longs for that. The light, the photons here, are like a constant blizzard. It makes him weary. It never stops. The deluge, the torrential downpour of photonic light. And these people, they are oblivious. Oblivious to so much.

"It's Danish," he says. That usually works.

"I see," says Kevan.

"Please carry on," says Autumn Blood.

He opens his eyes now. Kevan seems so far away through the storm of light. Yet he could put out this bony limb that he wears, and almost touch him. These twigs on the end of his arms. They call them fingers. He looks at them again. Every moment spent in this form is surreal. He moves his fingers and watches them dance at the end of his palm. Like leaves waving in the wind. Such fragility, he thinks, can cause so much violence.

He gets up and wanders over to the curtain. He opens it up. More light swims in like angry hornets. He looks outside. Behind him he clasps his hands together.

They are not that useful to him. He looks outside and there is the aftermath of carnage everywhere. It will take them a long time to rebuild he thinks. He looks at a smoke and fire licked car, practically a shell, now starting to rust in places. He picks it up with his mind and tosses it down the road. It tumbles on, head over heels like tumbleweed.

A lone woman, out on a walk watches it go by. She looks at the trees. Their limbs are still, their leaves are still. There is no wind about. She shrugs and walks on. Still, humans have no idea what has happened to them.

He turns around and looks at Kevan. Sitting there like a puppet. With one thought, the smallest amount of energy, he could be dead in an instant. Kevan looks at Autumn Blood looking at him, and he wonders about this strange reporter.

"It started on Remembrance Day or what used to be called Veterans Day here in the United States," says Kevan.

Kevan is tired. He looks at his arms. He can't remember them ever having fat and muscle on them. Now they are just twigs and gristle covered with a thin layer of skin. Smog comes up and bangs her head against his shin.

She is almost as thin as he is. He saved her from three teenagers. They didn't know what they were doing. In fact, he saved them too. Though they're probably dead by now. They wanted to eat her. There's still a lot of famine now.

Though a lot of folks have gone back to farming and some food is slowly making its way into towns and cities.

Kevan has no family. And he tries not to remember the times when he did. That just makes him sad. And crying on an empty stomach makes him feel sick. They live in apocalyptic times now. Some have called it the Great Wastetime. Others have called it purgatory. Mostly it's known as Wastetime, with or without the Great in front. Doesn't matter. It's the period after the few months that were known as Armageddon.

"You said you'd give me some food for the telling of my story," says Kevan. "Could I have a small bit now?"

He's trying his luck, but he hasn't eaten since yesterday, and his stomach growls. Autumn Blood comes over to where he was sitting and picks up the rucksack he had placed next to him. He puts his hand inside. There isn't anything in there, but he still pulls out an apple. It is large and green and shiny.

Kevan sees it. Saliva squirts inside his mouth and he swallows. He can almost smell it. Autumn Blood tosses it at him. It's a huge apple. He's never seen one so big.

It's gotta be the size of a grapefruit. He bites into it. The sweet and tangy flavor explodes with juice into his mouth. He thinks he might choke. He chews quickly and swallows. He bites again. His mouth is a sweet pool of cool, liquid love.

"Thanks."

Autumn Blood reaches into his empty rucksack and pulls out what looks like a raw chicken breast. Smog looks up at him. She paws at his legs. He smiles at her. He likes these little ones. These little brothers and sisters, better than the humans. He dangles it just above her nose. She swats at it with her paw. She meows. He lets it down lower and she jumps and bites it. He smiles at her.

"Enjoy little sister," he says.

She runs away with it into her kennel to enjoy the morsel. Autumn Blood looks at Kevan. His eyes are wide.

His mouth is slack and you can see his pink tongue like a piece of that raw pink chicken breast sitting behind his teeth.

"You... You..." Kevan gulps. He can't believe he's just seen this reporter give his cat meat.

"What Kevan?"

"You can't have meat," he says.

"It's not meat. It's cloned from a single cell that was taken eighteen months ago. It's well within regulations."

Kevan nods. He had heard about that, but he had never seen it. These regulations had been allowed because some of the species on earth were carnivorous. They needed flesh, until the genetic engineering would transform them to nourish on plants. Humans thought they were carnivores too. They since learned otherwise.

But it wasn't the flesh so much as the violence.

"Tell me how it began?" Autumn stands in front of him and watches him clutch his apple like it was his own beating heart. He hears Smog behind him purring as she eats her cloned flesh.

"We all call it Remembrance Day now because we don't want to forget. We can't forget. We'll die if we ever forget. We live in fear."

"There should be no fear. The rules are easy aren't they?"

"They are," nods Kevan. "But habits are hard to break for some people, and I still see some people drop dead now and then."

Autumn Blood nods. As they speak he can feel the thud of two human body's dropping dead. The heart is stopped. The knees forget what to do and the body crashes to the floor. The violence is silenced. The unnatural is put to an end. These two body's that are dead. What did they do? They were about to kill a rabbit.

The rabbit's nose was twitching. Its whiskers were trembling. It was cornered. The two had knives. It was a man and a woman. Autumn Blood could feel the fear behind the rabbits' eyes. He watched them, like the rabbit watched them, grab the rabbit by the throat.

The man was just about to slash the white furry throat. The woman holding the rabbit still for the man. His heart stops. Hers stops too. They're dead.

The rabbit looks for a moment before realizing he is free. He jumps over them and through a fence. He is gone in the thick brush of the field.

Autumn Blood smiles. You are safe little brother he thinks to himself. He looks at the dead bodies. He smiles again. That is a job well done.

"I remember I was walking along Times Square," says Kevan, "when all the screens flickered and went staticky to snow. Not many people noticed then, but in a manner of a few seconds, everything came to a halt...

Everything went quiet. Not just in Times Square or New York but around the world. It was eleven eleven pm Zulu Time. People who were sleeping were awakened. It was like you were watching a movie.

Somebody hit the pause button. We all just stopped, looked and listened.

Even those of us, so I heard, who weren't near a TV or radio heard the rules and regulations clearly. Like they were our own thoughts.

On the screens of Time Square a man came on. I can't describe him. Every time I try he keeps looking different, or like he's drifting away. Besides, those of us who tried to describe him couldn't keep it straight. Everyone seemed to have a different opinion of what he looked like. To this day, he's never been found."

Autumn Blood walked back to the window. He looked outside again. The woman wasn't out there anymore. She had moved on. This land had space again. There were far less vermin polluting it. Less bipedal bloodletters.

He looked back at Kevan. He was eating the apple core. When he was finished, and all he had left was the stalk, he started talking again. He twirled the stalk in his fingers like it was part of his hair. And long hair he did have. It was wavy and dark, like the color of that apple stalk, and it fell on his shoulders.

"You have to imagine. I tried to move, but I just couldn't," says Kevan. "It was the most surreal experience. Sort of like when you've just woken up from a dream and you know you're awake, you can see things and hear things but you just can't move. At least not for a few seconds. That's what it was like.

So this guy comes on to all the screens that I can see in Times Square and he starts talking. 'Earthlings,' he says, and I find that funny now. Actually, I found it funny at the time because he looked human and he didn't seem weird. He looked like he could've been an executive at some company, or bank even.

'We have grown weary of your arrogance.' This is him talking again, but he won't say who 'we' are. 'We have grown weary of your blatant disregard. We have grown weary of your callous disrespect of the breath of life. You have seventy two hours to halt the violence you perpetrate on this planet you are guests of.'

And that's exactly how he talks. Kind of weird, but at the same time he makes sense. That was the message.

That was all. Mostly, people ignored it, but I started to think about it. What does this guy mean by 'violence'? I mean, I understand it to a degree. Hitting someone or killing someone, that's obvious. That's violence. But what about spanking a child to correct their behavior. I mean, I was just thinking these sorts of things in my head.

Then the next day at exactly eleven eleven pm, pamphlets start falling from the sky. And when I mean sky, I mean, like if you were in your house, they'd just start falling from the ceiling. I was in my apartment. This apartment here. I was watching the eleven o'clock news and suddenly its raining papers in my apartment. And these pamphlets kept falling until my floors were covered with them about a quarter inch thick. At least three or four of these pamphlets thick.

I picked one up to read it, and this is what it said. '48 hours left to eradicate violence from Earth and from your hearts. To make it easier on you, this is what we mean by violence.

If anything moves on the land, moves in the air or moves in the water, DO NOT harm it. DO NOT harm yourself. Failure to abide by these rules will result in your immediate death.'"

Autumn Blood smiled. He remembered what those pamphlets said. He had practically written them. Through all the photons, through this constant barrage of light from their star, he could see those pamphlets still. They had helped. But many would perish in the months to come.

Smog came up to him, hopeful for more meat, more food. It wouldn't be long before this little carnivorous sister would be sustained on plants.

Kevan looked at Autumn Blood looking out the window. He looked somewhat familiar but maybe it was because he had a generic face. Hard to describe. He looked noble and youthful. But he was tired too. Not how he looked physically. No, that wasn't it. He looked tired in the emotional and spiritual way. He carried around an invisible weight that you could feel, intuitively.

Outside a group of young kids came into view. They were a gaggle of boys and girls. They were laughing and skipping. The lead boy held a ball. It was a good looking soccer ball. Made from leather. That meant it must've been more than eighteen months old. He dropped the ball and kicked it down the street. The kids ran after it.

Autumn Blood turned to Kevan. They smelled better now. Marginally. Not so much acrid, decaying flesh in their bodies anymore. Still, the specks of their ancestors floated around, imbuing everything with their acrid stain of violence. It would take years to get rid of it.

He blinked. These eye were strange. They got tired from looking. They dried and then these lids had to wipe them. So much undeveloped intelligence in this decaying body. He could see flakes of Kevan falling off him like waterfall cascades of skin. He could see the genetic clock winding down faster and faster in each of his cells. And as he sat there, a blank stare on his face, he sat dying. And he didn't even know it.

"Please continue Kevan."

"My friend Lawrence from down the hall came by the next day and we had a long talk about what this meant. He was one of the first to expire during the Cleansing as this man named it. Anyway, the day after these pamphlets fell, Lawrence came over totally happy. You see, he had been a vegan for three years at that point. And he said to me, 'see, I told you that we'd eventually have to stop this violence against Mother Earth and her helpless inhabitants.'

He was militant in his views, but he meant well. And our conversation got me thinking. The pamphlet had mentioned not to harm anything that moved on earth or in the water or in the air. I figured maybe he was right. I tried going vegan then."

"What happened to him?"

"Well it was the first evening of the Cleansing. Sometime after midnight on the fifteenth of November 2037. He and some buddies had decided that they were going to liberate laboratory animals.

They went round to this lab at the local university, and as they came into the holding room where they keep the animals, Lawrence saw this researcher in a white lab coat.

This guy was holding a rabbit on a table and on the table next to him, he was about to pick up a needle. I guess, from what I heard, Lawrence thought he was about to experiment on the rabbit so he took this club he had carried for protection and went to swing it at the guy. He dropped dead, right there. Lawrence did. This researcher was just going to administer a pain killer. He'd seen a couple of his colleagues drop dead that same evening as they were about to experiment on some animals.

Anyway, that was the beginning of the Cleansing. Now a lot of people will tell you that they didn't get enough warning, or the instructions weren't explicit enough. But they were. I mean there were one billion of us left after those first few months of the Cleansing. You didn't have to be an Einstein to figure it out. In any even there was another warning the next day after the first pamphlets."

Autumn Blood picked up Smog and sat back down. He could hear so much. All the voices all over the world. The children giggling, screaming and laughing down the road chasing the ball. The cacophony of sound. They didn't know how to shut up. These humans were hot air bags that whined and moaned and bellowed with each breath. Like the specks of light that kept raining down, their non-stop babble pelted him continuously. He could turn it off when he needed to. Like being stuck in a tin shack pelted constantly with pebbles. This is what the noise was like.

Little sister who sat on his lap purring. They were much better company. He rubbed her back, and she kneaded him with her claws.

"What did this second pamphlet say?"

"It was again at eleven elven that third night. This would've been the thirteenth of November 2037.

I was here in this apartment and these pamphlets started raining down again from the sky, or in my case from the ceiling.

I watched them fall down. It was weird, just as they started falling down, the ones from the previous night just seemed to vanish. A little bit like going up in smoke but it was such a small whiff, it was really hard to see. You had to watch closely for it.

I picked up one of these too. They were on incredibly thin paper, almost like an onion skin. I tried tearing it, but it wouldn't tear. I tried burning some after I had read them, but they wouldn't burn. Seemed like you couldn't destroy them."

"Do you have one to show me?"

Kevan shook his head. He tossed the apple stalk onto the living room table. It landed and spun around on some paper and books that were scattered on it.

"I wanted to keep one, and I tried, but it just vanished in a puff of smoke if you will. None of these magazines," he patted on the stack of magazines on his right, "no one in fact has been able to prove they even existed, except that what they said is burned into all of our memories.

There is no evidence. But collectively we have the memory. I can even see it now as if I was holding it in my hands, right now, right here."

Autumn Blood put Smog down on the floor. He put his hands back into his rucksack and pulled out a piece of raw steak. He gave it to Smog who hurried away into her kennel.

"That's fake too right?" Kevan asked. Autumn Blood nodded.

"Do you want some?"

"Um, no. I don't want to take my chances and I don't miss it anymore either."

Autumn Blood stuck his hands back into his rucksack. When he pulled them out his hand was holding a clear bag containing assorted nuts. It must have weighed a pound. Kevan instinctively licked his lips. Saliva filled his mouth again. Nuts were almost like currency. Such a dense food source was extremely valuable. What Autumn Blood was holding in his hands could be traded for everything he would need to live, except for food, for at least three months. Clothing, transportation, rent and utilities, you name it.

These humans as they call themselves, thought Autumn Blood, they are no better than their pets they used to belittle. Groveling for morsels of food, like common beggars. Autumn Blood put the open bag of nuts in his lap. He picked out a big Brazil nut and popped it in his mouth. Kevan stared at him greedily. He licked his lips again. He fidgeted with his hands. He bounced his knee quickly.

"Tell me what this pamphlet said," says Autumn, as he digs into his bag of nuts and flicks a large cashew at Kevan. Kevan puts it into his mouth and chews it quickly. Nothing has tasted so good for such a long time. He forgot what nuts had tasted like. He steals his glance away from the bag sitting in Autumn Blood's lap like a sack of gold coins.

"The second pamphlet said, '24 hours left to eradicate violence. If you do not eradicate violence, any violent act you attempt to commit will result in your swift and immediate death.

DO NOT harm any animals. DO NOT harm each other. DO NOT harm fish or birds. If you are in doubt then act according to the Golden Rule you have written about.

DO UNTO ANYTHING WHAT YOU WOULD HAVE DONE TO YOU.' That's all it said.

You have to understand that by now, some folks were becoming unhinged. There was rioting in many of the larges cities. London, Paris, New York, Toronto, Beijing. Practically any city that had more than a couple of million people had riots that started that night. Even here, in Detroit, which was half the city it had been just sixty years ago had riots.

The riots went on straight through the night. In the morning the army and coast guard had been called in. Same in other cities around the world. President Vera Sanchez here in the States practically begged for order. The thing is, the politicians were in denial. They didn't believe what was about to happen. I mean, I didn't either. But I had changed my diet by then. And on that third night it was getting easier. Folks were looting shops. Buildings were going up in flames."

Autumn Blood closed his eyes again slowly. In Nairobi two men were about to try to rape a woman walking home late at night. They had her pinned against an alley door.

The one man had a knife to her throat. The blade glinted in the moonlight like his wicked smile. The other man dropped his drawers. The he fell down. He hit the floor with a thud, a clump of brown flesh and messy clothes. The man with the knife dropped like a stone too. The woman looked at them. They lay lifeless. The knife spun on the dusty road a few times. Light glinting from the moon. She walked off hurriedly down the alley. She had heard of these things. Now she had seen it. These men's hearts had stopped beating before they hit the floor.

Autumn Blood was getting tired of this. He opened his eyes. Even after a year and a half, some of them wouldn't learn. Certainly things had slowed down. But he couldn't tell if it was because there were less of them now or because they were getting the message.

He reached into the bag and pulled out a handful of nuts. He tossed them in his mouth. He flicked an almond to Kevan.

"The next morning," droned on Kevan. Why was he doing this? Why was he listening to him when he knew what happened? It was tiresome.

"The army came. And all day and into the night they fought the rioters. They used rubber bullets and gas and water cannons. I watched a lot of it on television. It was the same everywhere. The politicians were getting angry. Many countries and cities had declared states of emergency.

I went downtown at around elven pm. I was curious you see. I wanted to know if this was some sort of hoax. I mean most of me believed it was a hoax. Really, who has that kind of power over life and death? But there was a small part of me that thought maybe, just maybe, this could be real.

Police everywhere were picking up suspects who seemed to be, or who kinda looked like the guy we had all seen on TV that one night. We never saw him again. The powers that be were promising that this was a huge hoax. They were saying that it was a group of hackers who had perpetrated this hoax. And they promised to get to the bottom of it. Authorities said it was tied to Islamic extremists. At least that's what we heard in the West. In the Middle East they blamed us. There was blame to be found everywhere.

Thing is, blaming it on a large international hack sounded good. It made sense. It gave some folks some sense of calm. But you just couldn't explain away these pamphlets that fell the second, and third night, and then just vanished.

You see, even as I was standing downtown on a side street, watching the city wage war with itself. Standing all over these pamphlets. At exactly eleven eleven pm, Zulu Time. I looked at my cell phone. At exactly that time, six eleven pm Detroit time, those pamphlets just disappeared in wisps of dust or smoke. Just like that. Bam, gone. Then... Then..."

Kevan trailed off. He looked at his lap. His bony hands clumped together like dry twigs. Autumn Blood tossed him a peanut. It landed in his lap. Kevan looked at it for a minute. Then took it and ate it. Smog was lying on the wooden floor, trying to sleep with eyes half open. Somebody walked by down the corridor. It was a young boy. He was twelve years old, living by himself now. His parents dead.

Autumn Blood watched him go by in his mind. He was disheveled and hungry. He would be dead within seven minutes, if he kept up with what was on his mind.

A slingshot was in his back pocket. Six iron ball bearings were in his front pocket.

Autumn Blood looked at Kevan. A tear rolled down Kevan's cheek. He pinched his trousers that covered skinny legs. They were frayed denim. Kevan looked away to his left. At the end of this living room he had a bookshelf. That's all he had. The only things of value. Electronics didn't work consistently. Computers were a luxury now that only the wealthy, and politicians could afford.

Autumn Blood watched Kevan swallow hard. The lump in his throat burning his heart. It was curious, these humans, capable of great compassion and yet such great violence.

He had never seen it before in all his many years of travel. His thousands of years of travel. Compassion had never been able to dwell in the same black heart as violence and hatred.

Yet here it was. The first time a black heart was found with compassion. It might be the only thing that saved them.

The boy with the slingshot walked out of the apartment complex and across the road into a field. There trees in the field and the grass came to his waist. A rabbit bounced off in fright. Autumn Blood watched the events unfold in his mind. Would this boy make the right choice. He didn't think so.

Kevan turned back to him and blinked his eyes. He dabbed at them with the hem of his shirt.

"Why do you want to know this?" he asked Autumn Blood.

"Because it is important that you remember." He tossed him another Brazil.

"Why aren't you recording it then?"

"I said it was important for you to remember, Kevan."

Kevan looked off behind Autumn Blood. On the wall behind Autumn Blood was an eight by ten landscape photograph of three people.

Kevan and his parents. It was taken in the summer of 2037. Mere months before the Cleansing had started. He'd tried to warn them to change their diet. But they wouldn't listen. Even with friends dropping dead around them they wouldn't listen.

That was the saddest part really. People dying for just a small piece of flesh. You can't really say that they were innocent. They'd been told not to eat animals. But they didn't understand. His parents didn't understand the violence inherent in it. It looked so innocent in white styrofoam trays with plastic covering. It wasn't an animal, it was just meat. It was easy not to think about it.

Kevan dabbed at his eyes again. They were stinging.

"Tell me about what you saw when it turned eleven eleven that fourth night."

Kevan looked back at Autumn Blood. Why was this guy so determined to have him relive the nightmare? If it wasn't for the promised food he'd tell him to fuck off.

Like petulant schoolchildren, thought Autumn Blood. They're practically destitute, it's still undetermined if they have the wherewithal to rebuild their society, and they carry around anger like hot leaden balls in their bellies. Even thought they brought this upon themselves.

"Well, like I was saying, I looked at my cell phone and at eleven eleven Zulu Time, the pamphlets just vanished. And then I heard this loud thumping or drumming sound and I looked up. There were hundreds of people rioting with police and all of a sudden it was like something invisible just knocked them on their ass. They just fell down. Both sides. Police and rioters. Probably ninety percent of them in that first ten or fifteen seconds. One guy next to me, he had a Molotov he was about to throw at the police, just dropped like a stone. Dead. I kicked the Molotov away and checked his pulse. Nothing there. Just lying dead. Just like that.

Then the police who were still alive came at the rioters and pandemonium broke out. The rioters started scattering and the police chased them down. As soon as they tired to grab a rioter.

Bam, the police fell down dead. As soon as a rioter tried to pick up a stone and fling it at the police, bam, same thing. Dead. Right in front of my eyes people keeling over dead like it was some big macabre hoax. I got scared and ran back to my apartment here."

"Do you want to know how many people died in those first eleven seconds after eleven eleven pm?"

"Not really," said Kevan, looking into his lap again.

"One hundred million."

And of course the numbers climbed from there, quickly and steadily, before tapering off after a few months as humans learned how to behave.

"Come with me to the window," said Autumn Blood.

He stood up and scooped his hand towards him, inviting Kevan to come with him. This method of communication was odd. He still hadn't got used to it.

The gestures, the moving of the mouth and lips to make sounds.

So many sounds. So many words. So many languages. It was tedious and archaic.

Perhaps that was the reason for their problems. Lack of clear and thoughtful communication. They didn't understand each other. And misunderstandings led to hurt feelings and hurt feelings led to violence.

He looked out the window again. He blinked his eyes slowly, adjusting to the light. Photons streaming everywhere, a cascade, a waterfall of light.

Kevan came up and stood close to him. Almost touching. Autumn Blood thrust his head up and down in the direction of the field outside.

"What do you suppose that boy is going to do?"

Kevan looked out across the road and into the field. A torso was running, bobbing up and down like a buoy in the field of tall grass. The boy came upon a line of trees and stopped. He cocked his head up and at an angle. He scanned the canopy, listening.

"What do you suppose he's going to do?" Autumn Blood asked again.

Kevan looked. He saw the slingshot in his back pocket. The boy was probably a hundred feet away, but he could see the Y. He could see the rubber band and pocket swaying slowly, like a smile.

"Uh... Um, he's probably going to climb those trees and look for fruit."

That's not what he really thought the boy would do. That's what he wanted him to do. Life had become so expendable. He didn't want it that way anymore. It should be precious. But the way people were dying. Dropping dead like autumn leaves in a cold wind was unbearable. It lay heavy upon his soul like a thick, cold blanket of snow.

"Saying it, does not make it so," said Autumn Blood. He doesn't turn to look at Kevin. He's watching that twelve year old boy wrestle with his thoughts.

He's not even wrestling with his conscience and that's the shame. He's wrestling with how many iron balls it'll take to make a kill.

How he's gonna defeather the bird, and how he's gonna make a fire to eat it. He's not even worried about the ethical consideration.

Hell, he's not even thinking about the rules. How he'll be dead before he makes his mark.

This is the shame of these bipedals, thinks Autumn Blood. Like amoeba they're driven by base instincts. When they're hungry enough, no higher consciousness comes into play.

"The problem with you," Autumn Blood says to Kevan, but he's not talking about Kevan specifically, but about humanity, "is that you don't think. You get hungry enough and you leave all conscience behind. You leave all philosophy behind. This boy over there is just thinking about how he might cook this bird. He's forgotten that he won't even get that chance. The incredible thing is, he's not even asking the right questions. I get it. He's hungry. But the question he should be asking is what are the birds eating? What is that rabbit he passed eating? You have a long way to go Kevan. A very long way to go. And I don't even know if you'll make it. In eleven seconds this boy will be dead."

Kevan stares outside. His mouth opens wide. His eyes don't blink. Don't do it, please don't do it, he thinks, speaking to the boy.

"Nine seconds."

Autumn Blood is a statue. His arms are clasped behind his back. He'd sooner not have them. These limbs are encumbrances for him. They are like unwieldy sticks stuck to his person. Damn annoying, dangling baubles.

Kevan watches the boy pull the slingshot from this back pocket. He holds it in his left hand. He pulls out an iron ball from his right front pocket with his right hand. Kevan sees it glint in the sunlight as he puts it into the pocket of the slingshot.

The light is like shards of glass. Billions of pieces of shards of glass. Autumn Blood longs for the darkness of space. The solitude, the quietness. How long must he endure this wasteland. This Great Wastetime as the humans now call it. He will serve his tour. His punishment with gallantry.

Kevan brings up his hand to his mouth. He covers it. He wants to scream out but the boy won't hear him. The windows are closed and the boy is too far away.

"Four seconds," says Autumn Blood. This is happening too often now, he thinks.

Perhaps there is too much hunger, and yet there is still enough food.

It's just not getting to them. He can help. But he is not supposed to. He's not even supposed to give Kevan the help he's offered.

The boy outside steadies the slingshot and takes aim. He pulls the rubber band along his left arm and away towards his right shoulder. He's looking for the bird.

"Goodbye," says Autumn Blood.

The boy falls straight down. The iron ball is released, harmlessly into the field just a few feet away. The boy falls as if he fell into a hole in the ground. What happened is his heart just stopped. Just like that.

"God damn," says Kevan. Now he blinks his eyes. The feral dogs come. They've learned to wait for the dead.

They tried the killing too, but killing is not allowed. Not by any who move upon the land or in the air or in the sea.

Even the lion must wait patiently, hungrily, for death's hand upon his prey, rather than try to kill as he has always done.

The thing is, the animals learned this quickly. Unlike the humans.

Autumn Blood turns to Kevan. His hands are still clasped behind his back.

"Tell me about your parents," he says.

They both go back to sit down. Kevan is tempted to grab the bag of nuts and run out of there. He's not liking his guest anymore. He doesn't think he's a reporter. But he's scared. He sits down fidgeting with his hands. Autumn Blood passes him the bag of nuts.

"Talk to me," he says.

Kevan chooses a nut carefully. He digs around in the bag with skeletal fingers until he finds a filbert. He pops it into his mouth. He closes up the bag carefully. He must protect these, let them last. They are like gold to him.

"I came home that night. The fourteenth of November at just before midnight. My parents were watching the TV. I came in and saw all the dead bodies. Piles of them everywhere. We stayed up almost all night. The next morning was Sunday morning. My parents always made brunch with eggs and toast and bacon and sausages.

My mother called me down to brunch. It was just after eleven in the morning. She served us up a plate of food. I told her no, that we couldn't eat the meat and eggs. Nothing from animals, I said. Didn't she remember the pamphlets. I begged her, I begged my father. Please don't. Just the toast. Just the orange juice. They wouldn't listen. I can still see them now, putting a forkful of bacon and sausage on their fork. Together, like they were going to prove something to me..."

Kevan looked into his lap and a tear fell from his cheek and landed on the bag. It looked like a blister.

"And then they put their forks to their mouths. Watch this Kevan, my father said to me, see, and he put the fork into his mouth. My mother too. They fell face first into their plates of food. The forks still stuck in their mouths like silver serpent tongues."

He was crying now. He looked at Autumn Blood. His eyes were swollen and wet. The rims were red and his sclera was ribboned with red blood vessels. Clear, wet worms of tears streamed down the middle of his cheeks, dropping like bombs into his lap.

"Who are you really?" he asked, looking at Autumn Blood.

Can You Please Be Quiet

The soldier is sitting on a box of grenades. His rifle, a dusty M16, is lying dead next to him on the dusty ground. It is hot outside. He takes his helmet off his head and drops it on the ground. It spins and wobbles in front of him. His gloved hands rub his head, his curly brown hair.

"They've gotta let me go. Goddammit they've gotta let me go," he says.

Spit drops from his mouth and a bubble of snot can't make up its mind if it's coming or going from his nose. His eyes are bloodshot and wet. The box of grenades is locked and he's dragged it out into the open from storage. He shouldn't have done that. But he needs someplace to sit. His face is stained with oil, dust and sweat. A river of sweat snakes down the side of his cheek by his ear. It caresses the curve of his jaw and sneaks under his undershirt.

"It's too goddamn hot here," he says.

He's still rubbing his head, a fine mist of salty sweat sprays up like a halo. He rubs the backside of his gloved knuckles into his eye sockets.

He's trying to get rid of the dampness, the sting and the scratchiness of this Arab air. The heat makes breathing hard. It's chokingly hot. He's been here four months already. Two more and he might get home. Might.

Word on the street, though, is that they could see their tours doubled. Twelve months is too long. He won't last that long. He might not last another day. Every day is a tour. A grinding tour.

He can't stomach food anymore. This soldier. Everything is salted with sand. Disgusting, hot, sweaty sand of these hell's acres.

"We're heading out, Riley," says a colleague.

He gets up. He sighs and takes a deep breath. He looks out through the barbed wire fence. Way out in the distance to the city. The city in ruins. Must he go there again? He goes there everyday to look and see. To prod and prick. To find what can be uncovered. Everyday is another disaster. A day spent in this oven. He wipes his forehead. He pulls a red bandana out of his pocket and ties it over his head. It starts to sop up his sweat.

He grits his teeth.

"Fuck," he says under his breath.

He picks up his helmet and puts it on. Then he puts on his goggles. They help with the sun. It's bright out here. The sun is an interrogation. A burning cigarette deep in his mind. The headaches won't go away. And his body can't escape the headaches. He looks at the Humvee. He hates riding in that tin can. He looks down for his M16 and picks it up. He smacks the butt of it with his gloved hand. The dust billows up and off.

His colleague is in the Humvee already. He has started it up. He walks over and gets into the front passenger seat. He doesn't put on his seatbelt. That is the least of his worries. This soldier has a hundred other ways he'd rather die.

A colleague jumps into the back. He carries a radio pack. Riley gives the order to roll out. The driver steps on the gas and the wheels spit dust and gravel out the back towards the camp. Then the tires grip and they move. The security gate is lowered and they're out in the open. Vulnerable. A can of sardines.

Riley looks up out the window. A heli is coming back towards base.

It's a thirty minute drive into the city in ruins. Everyone, it seems, wants to kill them. The soldier is looking out the window. He's watching the acres of desert with their rippling waves off in the distance. Not a single cloud in the sky. It's a baby blue. Though there aren't many babies around these parts. Not the living ones anyway.

The soldier thinks of his baby. She's three months old now. He hasn't seen her. Not in real life. Not how it matters. He puts his hand into his shirt and pulls out a locket. It's small and made of gold plated something. It's rectangular, like a very small book. A little smaller than the dog tags that cover it up. He pushes them aside and opens up the locket.

A young woman, she looks maybe twenty, is on one side. That picture is a few years old. On the other side is Melissa. That is his daughter. She's two months old in the picture. She's smiling. Her blues eyes are open. They're like stolen pieces of this sky. She's in someone's arms. Her mother's arms. The soldier rubs her face with his gloved thumb.

His eye's sting again. He shuts them and thinks of a little patch of green. It is the smallest green he's ever owned. It's his backyard in Iowa. The small piece of land he owns. Where things live. Where things grow. Like the tulips his wife plants every spring.

Red tulips. Those petals of blood. He's seen a lot of blood. Lots of blossoming blood in these parts. When it rains, it's blood rain. He's lost three colleagues. This driver here next to him is new. He's only known him three weeks. That guy behind him. The one that just won't shut the fuck up, has been around the same time he has.

He doesn't want to see blood anymore. He hates the sight of it. He can't eat flesh anymore either. And he craves steak. But it makes him puke. The metallic, damp smell of blood has stained his nostrils. He can't quit it. Red is everywhere. In the rusty dust, like flecks of red, glint like scabs.

Jarrod C. Goldberg is driving. His gaze is steady. He just grunts now and then. He's nineteen. Thinks this is an adventure. But he's only been here three weeks.

He hasn't seen shit. Juan F. Paez is radiohead. He sits in the back and won't shut up. Will you please be quiet, thinks the soldier. Juan talks because if he's talking he's alive. He thinks so long as he talks he'll live. Maybe he's onto something.

Julian L. Riley is commander. He's only a specialist. Specializing in killing people. They're supposed to be a fireteam but there's only the three of them. All three jokers, a pack of three js. It's not funny.

"Is that your missus?" asks Paez, tapping the soldier on his shoulder.

Riley nods, looks back down at his two girls and then closes the locket. He slides the dog tags carefully over to protect it. One on top, one underneath. He puts it back inside his shirt. It rests on his sternum. Not far from his beating heart. The blood pump. The pumping red chamber.

"I got me a missus back home. Can't wait until we're outta here, right, TL. I'm gonna fuck my missus like she wants it. Man, that's gonna be good times. Just eight more weeks, TL, eight more weeks. Woohoo."

TL is team leader. That's what he is, our soldier. A team leader. A leader who has led three men to their deaths. He doesn't like to get close no more. Not to anyone. Can't remember why he joined up for this death march. Thought the idea of sun and sand sounded like fun. But this isn't the goddamn beach, soldier. That should've been the first clue. When they told him that. Yeah, plenty of sand and sun. None of which makes for leisure.

In fact, our soldier hates the sand. It gets everywhere. Right up in your butt crack even when you're fully clothed. And sometimes even after a shower you'll still find sand stuck to you like fleas. Or you're rubbing your face and you can't tell if you've got a five o'clock shadow or the sand has caked dry after sticking itself to you through your sweat.

He wipes his forehead. The sweat is leaking out under his bandana. These army fatigues are heavy. The flak jacket makes it worse. You can't take a good breath of air. Like a corset. Tight around you like a python. Unlike a lover's embrace.

"You guys, take a look at Maria," says Paez.

He pulls out a picture the size of his palm from his front breast pocket. He thrusts it into the front of the cabin, between Goldberg and our soldier. Riley looks over at it. He nods. Goldberg glances it at it too. The edges are curled and frayed. Paez has been looking at it a lot.

"Nice," says Goldberg.

He looks back at the unending desert. The gold brick road some of the boys call it. Irony. That's what they say. There's no goddamn gold here. But the gold brick road they call it anyway. We're not in Kansas anymore. No shit, Charlie.

Goldberg is a Jew. He told Riley this was his Jihad. Guess they don't have a word for that in Israeli. Riley thinks he's a schmuck. Everybody over here is a schmuck as far as he's concerned. He's the biggest schmuck of them all. This is his second tour and he'll likely do a third. If he lasts that long.

Like being trapped in an abusive relationship. Paez takes his picture back. Looks at Maria's face and kisses it.

"Te quiero," he says.

Goldberg grits his teeth. They have to slow down some because the road is so goddamn bad. There are potholes everywhere. The ride is not comfortable. This is a military vehicle. The hum fucking vee. Like riding a bucking bronco sometimes.

"So what are we gonna do out there in the city in ruins, TL?" Paez asks.

Our soldier doesn't say anything. He's gone back to looking out the window. He's watching his life slide by like the grains of the sand outside. Millions of them. Tick tock. Tick tock. Tick tock.

Paez puts his hand on our soldier's shoulder and shakes it. Riley flinches.

"What are we looking for, TL?" he asks again.

"Peace and quiet," says Riley. "Some peace and quiet."

"Not me," says Goldberg, "I want to kill me some Ahabs."

Riley's still looking out the window. He wonders what the barrel of his rifle tastes like. Gunpowder. That's gotta be salty. Maybe salt and pepper.

"Dude, you obviously haven't been in a fire fight," says Paez, "it isn't a whole lotta fun. Once, when TL and I were out here, we got ambushed. We lost two fucking men. Remember that, TL? Two of the best men I ever met. Yeah we cut up some Ahabs, but it wasn't fun. No man, it wasn't fun at all. Was it, TL?"

Riley shakes his head slowly. Not fun. That's a strange word in a strange country. Such a small word. Three letters. Like sun. Fun in the sun. Hell no, there isn't any fun in this sun. This is like hell's armpit. Hot and sweaty and stinks of shit.

"Get me a water, J," says our soldier. He's talking to Paez.

Paez reaches into a cooler next to him and pulls out a bottle of water. He passes it to Riley. Riley opens it up and tosses the cap on the floor between Goldberg and him. He drinks all of it. Sixteen ounces and tosses the bottle in the middle of the floor.

They pass a fireteam coming back the other way. This gold brick road is sometimes busier. Today it's pretty quiet.

That's the first friendly they've seen in the fifteen minutes they've been driving. They're halfway there.

Their job is reconnaissance. Look for anything suspicious. Radio it in if they see anything and hang tight if they're caught in a fire fight.

"Man, I still think of Bones. You remember him, TL? He was one skinny mother fucker. Just skin and bones." says Paez.

Paez keeps talking. Can't shut the fuck up. Our soldier remembers Bones. He was a small thin black guy with a big smile. He was from Arkansas. Benton, Arkansas. Yeah, that's right. You couldn't get Bones down. He didn't like it here. But he was fighting for freedom. It was the fight for right. That's what he always said. Fight for right. Fight for your right to party. That's what the guys in the platoon would tease him with. He didn't mind. You couldn't upset him. "Nah," he'd say grinning, "fight for right. Bring freedom to these people."

"And then one afternoon. It was so hot. Hotter than today right, TL? Hotter than hell. It was a day spent in hell.

We got stuck in a shit storm man. Jesus, these fuckers just come out of nowhere. Like vomit out of a dog's belly. Just bam, bam, bam..." Paez carries on.

Our soldier remembers him. They were on foot, they'd been dropped off inside the city in ruins. They came out into an open courtyard and that's when it happened. Arabs coming out of every orifice the building had. Pistols, rifles, even one idiot came at them with a shafra. A knife. Bones putting a couple of poppies on him. Nice red poppies just about around the heart. He dropped onto the stone. They ran to take cover in a small alcove.

The rattle of gunfire was loud. It was enhanced by the courtyard. Chunks of paint and stone came off around them as the Arabs rained lead. They took cover for a while. Waiting, trying to watch. But they couldn't wait long. Our soldier Riley, slid out just a hair, looking. He took sight of an Arab as gunfire spat at him. He got hit on the temple with a splinter of plaster and rock. It cut and he bled. But he zipped off a few rounds. He got his Arab. He fell down. Dead.

He didn't feel anything. In his mind, he didn't feel anything. Killing that Arab. It felt like a game. He didn't really give a shit. He didn't feel bad about it. But he wasn't happy either. He just hated this place. Moving here, baking in hell's oven.

"He took one for the team. He didn't even think about it. He just did it, man. Fucking courage. He got a Purple Heart for it too. His wife will get it. Probably has it already by now," says Paez.

"Purple Heart ain't gonna sing his baby a goodnight lullaby," says Riley.

Paez stops for a second. Looks at our soldier but then carries on talking.

"Nah, TL, it won't. But man, he deserved it. I never seen courage like that..." says Paez.

Yeah, courage for sure. He took a grenade for them. All of them. There were four of them that day. They called in air when they got ambushed, but it took a couple of minutes for the Apache to arrive. By that time Bones had been cut to ribbons by the grenade. Looked like someone had scooped out his belly with a big metallic orange squeezer.

At least he didn't suffer. That's what they say. Like it's supposed to be of comfort or something like that. There's no comfort in war. There are no winners either. Just one side of losers and a bigger side of losers.

Bones had jumped up on that grenade. Clutched it to his belly like he'd caught an overtime touchdown. Our soldier turned him over after the thump and slight hump of his body as the grenade exploded underneath him. He turned him over and he had no hands.

Just stumpy ends of meat where his wrists were. Looked like they had melted into the scooped out part of his belly. Just a mess of wet fatigues, black and red burnt and minced flesh.

Even now Riley feels the need to heave. He stops himself. Swallows hard. Comfort my ass, he thinks. There's no comfort in dying quick. No comfort in dying period. Not when the heavy baggage is left for others to carry. The fucking dead weigh a ton. We all carry them around, he thinks. Their remains are heavy. Balls and chains of death and dismemberment.

After the Apache came in and tore the courtyard to shreds and everyone inside of it except the three of them who were living, they sent in Medevac. Should've been the coroner. Bones was long dead. His eyes long turned to glassy marbles.

"That Bones, man I miss him. Hey, TL? Wasn't he just the greatest? He always had a smile on his face. You couldn't get the dude upset. Smiles is what some of us called him, though Bones is what most called him. He was like the only goddamn ray of sunshine in this hellhole." says Paez.

Nothing lives in this wasteland. Not even clouds. At least not often. Riley's looking out front now. You can see the city in ruins coming up on the horizon. It's wavy. The heat of the sand makes it look almost like a mirage. But he's been down this gold brick road over a hundred times. He used to count. But a hundred is a long time. Doing it almost every day, it takes a while. So he knows he's getting close to the bowels of hell again.

You can look up in the sky for a hundred miles in any direction and see nothing. No birds. Nothing wants to be here.

The goddamn city doesn't want to be here. It's hell bent on destroying itself. And they'll help it along. Some of the small things that live here, like scorpions and snakes. They'd sooner kill you than look at you. Same with the Arabs. But that's mutual. Sometimes our soldier would sooner kill them than look at them. And that's the God's honest truth. That's what he would say.

But he doesn't like to say much. His mind rambles on and on at him, all the time. Droning on and on. There is no peace and quiet anymore. None. He stares ahead. He tunes out Paez and swims deep within his own murky mind. The place is a cesspool. He knows that. Scum grows inside it. That's the only thing that can in this place. But at least he can swim deep in it and get lost. Step away from his body's reality sometimes.

He likes the Jew. At least Goldberg is quiet. He's a schmuck, but aren't we all, he thinks. At least he's a quiet schmuck. Like our soldier. It's easier not to know someone when they're quiet. Small mercies. Small fucking mercies.

He'd be able to forget Goldberg quicker than Bones. He'd forget Goldberg quicker than Paez. You get to know people by speaking with them. Communicating. That's how you form bonds. So he doesn't communicate much anymore. Only when he has to. Like when they reach the city he'll radio it in.

Our soldier wants life to be easier. He doesn't like complications. Maybe that's why he doesn't like the war too much. It's complicated. It's complicated having to think first and not shoot first. He'd sooner shoot first, ask questions later. But that's not how he's been raised. That's not how the good guys do it.

These Arabs. They don't ask questions. So things are easier for them. They'd sooner shoot you than look at you. And they do. He's seen it more times than not. He rubs his nose. It's itchy. Already it's caked in sand. Looking behind him he sees the plume of dust like big balloons. Here we are they say. Look at us. We're coming. Could have a guy on the rooftop just waiting. Licking his lips as he steadies his RPG.

It could happen. Every goddamn day is either a gift or a death sentence.

You never know. But they're getting closer. Our soldier pulls out some binoculars from the cubby. He holds them to his eyes. He scans the city's outer buildings. Nothing higher than five stories. He doesn't see anyone standing on the rooftops.

That's usually a good sign. Not always. You could have your guy up there with his RPG, crouching below the short wall that wraps around the rooftop. You've gotta keep vigilant. And it's the vigilance that's ruining him. He can hardly sleep anymore.

Sometimes these Arab faces are all sneering at him. He wants to wipe the smirks off their faces. His colleagues are smirking at him too. Everywhere he looks. Faces are jeering and the lips are curling in cruel irony. As if to say they have his number. And it's up.

Goldberg slows down to twenty miles an hour as they come up on the last half mile stretch to enter the city in ruins. Nobody can be seen around. That's not unusual.

Most of the citizens that live here have moved into the center of the city. You can't blame them. There's more shelter there when the fighting starts.

Our soldier is still scanning the horizon but he's got a better look now. He sees a couple of dogs trotting along the outer perimeter. They're bony. Hungry. Like he is. Hungry to get back home. If they'll ever let him leave this place. Up on the rooftops he doesn't see anything. It makes him more nervous than if he saw an Arab up there with an RPG. It shouldn't, but it always does. It's the surprise attacks that are overworking his adrenals. He can't relax anymore. Always, his ears are pricked to any sounds.

If only Paez would shut up. He could hear things. Maybe not. The Humvee is growling underneath him, like a hungry beast. Everyone is so goddamn hungry in this godforsaken stretch of desert.

The dogs are hungry for food. The Arabs are hungry to get rid of the Americans. And folks like Bones are hungry to bring peace. Riley's hungry to get the hell out of there.

His mind can't be trusted anymore. He hears things. Voices taunting him. If only they'd be quiet. Please be quiet, he says in his mind.

It's hard enough to deal with the voices when Paez keeps droning on and on. He's like a wind up toy that natters incessantly.

"Okay Goldberg, this is where we have to stay focused. Gotta keep your eyes scanning about. When we enter the shitty in ruins, there're tons of alleys and doorways and windows where these fuckers could be hiding, just looking for a chance to light us up. Hard to tell who is the friendly and who are the terrorists, so be careful. Isn't that right, TL?"

Our soldier doesn't say anything.

"Paez, I'm fucking driving here, I can't do everything. You're gonna have to keep eyes sharp. If we take fire and you don't warn us, I'm blaming you," says Goldberg.

"I'll do my best, but I'm in the back here. It's harder to see. TL's got a great view. He sees stuff too. Right, TL?"

"Less talking and more watching," says our soldier.

They're closer now and Riley takes the binoculars from his eyes. He puts them away. He takes hold of his M16 and rests it between his legs. Where it was before, but this time he's holding onto it tighter. It's like his rod of reality. It's the only thing that keeps him sane.

They enter the mouth of the city in ruins. It engulfs them. It's claustrophobic, he can hardly breath in these small spaces. The road narrows. It'll barely allow two vehicles side by side. Certainly not two Humvees. The shadows play tricks everywhere. Our soldier looks around. He's on tenterhooks. He grips the barrel of his rifle harder than it needs. He puts his right hand down to feel the thickness of his Beretta's holster. He pats the magazines on his chest. He's got lots of ammo. That makes him feel ever so slightly more comfortable.

Sweat is snaking down his cheeks. He doesn't notice this now. He's looking around. It's eerily quiet. They're crawling along at about ten miles an hour. They might as well be sitting ducks.

A young boy runs out of a door in front of them. They all flinch.

Our soldier can't get his rifle up. The distance is too close between him and the windshield. He doesn't like this part. The drive up, before they exit the Humvee to travel on foot. It's a give and take. You take away the bullet proof enclosure of the Humvee, but you gain mobility. He prefers it that way.

"Call it in," he orders Paez.

"Delta Base, this is Fireteam Riley. We have entered the city," says Paez into his mic.

"Copy that Fireteam Riley. Play safe."

"Pull up around the corner there and park," says Riley to our driver.

Just around the corner they come out into an opening, it's the main market area of the city in ruins. It's about the size of a football field. It's the place to park and start off on foot. Goldberg pulls up behind an abandoned and burnt up van. They're right in the middle of the market. Out in the open.

"Fuck no, Goldberg. Pull us up someplace safe. Jesus man, you want us to make it through this goddamn day?"

It's a rhetorical question. Our soldier points off to the side of an abandoned building. There is rubble several feet from the side of the building, it makes a half-assed alcove. It should help provide some protection. Goldberg drives up to it.

"Back in, so we can get out quicker," says Riley.

There's no one in this open market. It's late in the afternoon. The sun will set in an hour. They'll be long gone by then. Well on their way back to Delta Base. The evening trips into the city in ruins always had air support alongside.

"We've got a half hour to see if we can find any insurgent activity out in that block of the city," says Riley.

He's pulled out a map of the city in ruins. He's pointing out the window to their right. Paez is leaning in from the back seat. Goldberg is leaning in over the middle. Riley puts his finger on the map.

"This is where we are. We're gonna head up here, zig zag around like this," he's gesturing with his finger, tracing a maze through the streets.

"Then we'll double back this way, here," he says.

His finger comes back to their starting point. It's a loop of about a two thirds of a mile.

"We're not banging down doors. This a recon patrol. If we get activity we go in after it. Other than that we're walking the street and acting friendly. Understood?" asks Riley.

"Hell yeah, TL," says Paez.

Goldberg nods his head.

"I want fucking peace and quiet on this. There hasn't been activity in a couple of days and that makes me nervous. Quiet as fucking church mice, okay? Paez?" says Riley.

Paez pinches his thumb and forefinger together and drags them across his mouth.

"Not a word from me, TL," he says.

They exit their Humvee and take formation. Our soldier is in the front and Paez with the radio is in the back. They drop in behind the rubble and scan the market.

They take their time with this. Our soldier is jumpy. He's overly cautious. He scans thoroughly. He has a bad feeling about this. He always has a bad feeling. But this time it's a really bad feeling. Every time it's a really bad feeling. He can't trust his instincts anymore. The goddamn voices in his head are making him mad.

They start their walk along the dirty, white colored wall. They walk close to it to protect themselves from any fire. Though they are exposed for a hundred feet until they turn right, up the street. They stay close to the wall on the right side of the street. Our soldier glances up and down the road. He looks up at the roofs. He stops and glances quickly into alcoves and recessed doors before moving on past them.

It is quiet. Eerily quiet. He hears the maddening voices. The voices that keep repeating liked looped tape. You'll never get out of here alive, soldier. You're gonna die a young man. Your wife will live as a widow and your child end up fatherless.

He can't stop them. He swats them away like black flies. But there are many of them.

They buzz around incessantly in the sewer that is his mind. This place has created his insanity. This killing. The blood and the bodies. The broken, the severed bodies. Things that no man should ever see. He has seen these things. They fester like maggots in the open sores created in his mind.

The ooze of crazy seeps and drips daily into his empty skull. He lives in internal images of violence. The stench of his own mind. It is overpowering. He wants to put an end to it. If you can make it through these next eight weeks. He'll go AWOL. He'd sooner end up in jail than back here.

He fumbles in his breast pocket for a pill. The doctor has given it to him for anxiety. He pops the small white pill and chews it. It tastes slightly bitter. It hardly has any effect anymore. He wonders if it is a sugar pill. A placebo. His heart bangs in his chest. His ribs grip his lungs like a vice.

He looks down and watches ants crawling along the ground. The three of them like ants crawling along the ground. He steps on them, but he doesn't squash them. They escape into the crevices of his boot's soles.

Goldberg is looking around. He's got his finger on the trigger of his M16. That's not how he's supposed to carry the rifle. He knows that. But it makes him feel more secure. Why waste time slipping your finger into the loop when you could be there anyway. His finger is itchy. An itchy trigger finger.

Paez is talking to himself in his own mind. He's counting steps, counting windows as they pass by. He tries not to step on cracks in the road. It's hard. This place is full of cracks. His rifle is pointing off to the left and down. His finger is outside the trigger. But he keeps moving it around the trigger loop. Reminding himself where it is. Just in case.

They turn right down a smaller alley. No cars can drive down here. It is perhaps three feet across. Our soldier feels squashed.

He can't breathe. He tries to take a deep breath but his ribs grip harder around his lungs. His heart is hammering. Flailing about like a large fish in the empty space of his chest. His throat is dry. He can't swallow.

There is nothing to swallow. Up ahead, five feet, is a door.

A wooden, battered door. He can hear some Arabic and laughter coming through it. Something catches his eye, glinting off the sun. He looks up to see a figure move out of sight up on the roof. He can't be sure if it was real or if he imagined it. He puts his fist up. His colleagues stop behind him. He points up to the left, towards the roof.

He moves them into the doorway. They crouch down. Our soldier can hear himself breathing. It sounds like a deep wind coming in from the desert. They wait and watch. Keeping an eye up at the roof. A grenade comes down from the roof above them. It bounces like a can towards them. Riley runs up to it and kicks it down the road from where they came. He runs back towards the door where his colleagues are. Machine gun fire erupts around him. He hears the whizz and the bang and the crunch of bullets ricocheting and tearing up the road. He leans up hard against the door.

The bang of the grenade is loud. It deafens him for a moment. Shrapnel whizzes past, embeds itself in the wall to his right and the wooden window frames.

A small piece rips carelessly across his right bicep. It's just a flesh wound. He winces. It hurts.

They're somewhat exposed. Riley fires his M16 up at the roof. The Arabs duck down. They take this time to run across the alley. Goldberg hammers his shoulder against a door. It splits open easily and he stumbles in. They run through a hallway. They see civilians in their periphery. They run up the stairs to the second floor. They run more stairs to the rooftop. Riley stops them. They stand to the side. Pressed against the walls. He listens. He hears footsteps outside on the rooftop.

He opens the door and slips out to the right. Goldberg slips out to the left. Paez is out right behind Riley. Riley sees two young men. Hell, they could be teenagers. They have AK-47s. They're turning around from looking over the rooftop, scanning for where our soldiers came from.

Riley opens fire. So does Goldberg. Chips of stone and plaster puff off the wall behind the Arabs. Puffs of red erupt from their chests. They drop to their knees and then fall face first to the ground.

Riley and Goldberg and Paez walk up to the two Arabs. They kick the rifles away, looking down at the two dead bodies.

Behind a stone wall rises a young boy. Maybe he's twelve. He's got an AK-47 in his hand too. He catches them by surprise. Riley flinches and yanks on his trigger as he brings his M16 up. The bullets sew into the roof as his rifle works its way up inline with the boy. The rooftop explodes in little puffs of dust and smoke. The bullets needle up until they bite into flesh. Six, maybe more pieces knit into the boy as his body goes limp and he falls back behind the wall as if he wasn't there.

Something bites at Riley's heel. His leg gives out. He drops to his knee and turns around. An old man with a gray beard is letting his pistol rip. Goldberg is turning around when Riley sees him take one in the face. Right through the cheek. It looks like someone squashed a ripe tomato on his face. Goldberg does a face plant on the roof. Dead.

Another bullet rips through our soldier's trapezius. His left arm is almost numb.

He lifts up his rifle with his right hand. Fuck, it's heavy he thinks. Heavier than he remembers. He pulls the trigger and a spurt of bullets kick out of the muzzle. Then click. Nothing. Click. Nothing. Riley looks down at his M16. The magazine is empty. He uses his numb left arm to fumble for a clip. The old man is staggering towards them. He pulls the trigger on his pistol, but he's empty too.

Paez opens fire. He empties his magazine into the bearded man. Splotches of red dot his abdomen and chest. Half his face gets torn off before he falls down in a pile of messy clothes.

Paez comes up to our soldier. He helps him reload a clip into the M16. He helps him up. He can stand on his right leg, but it hurts like a wasp sting. Paez helps him back to the door they entered the roof from. Our soldier limps down the stairs. They round the corner on the second floor. A small boy cowers by the curtain. He's holding something. Riley opens fire, he sews red buttons haphazardly across the boy's chest. They boy stops moving. A toy car falls out of his hand.

"Mother fuckers," yells our soldier, "they all wanna kill us."

He's not making much sense. His mind's gone AWOL from his body. They come down the stairs to the first level. There's a woman in a burqa yelling and screaming and crying at them. Riley cuts her down.

She falls down in a lump of black fabric. He steps on top of her and over her as they walk outside.

"Take it easy," says Paez. "I'll get you back, TL. Hold tight, man."

Riley's eyes are wide and glassy. There are some men and women standing around the doorways, outside in the alley, when they exit.

"What the fuck are you looking at!" shouts Riley.

He empties another clip at them. Spraying bullets up and down the alley.

"TL, take it easy," says Paez.

He's yelling something into his radio. Riley can't make sense of it. All he hears are the voices in his head. They hobble down the alley back onto the main street.

Riley can't feel anything. They make it back out into the open market. They run as best they can for the Humvee. They see the Black Hawk coming from far off. The helicopter blades thudding in the sky like a deep heartbeat. The Black Hawk settles down in the market. Four marines exit and they come up to him.

"I've gotta get outta here," he says. "You've gotta let me get outta here."

He's not making sense. They want to know where Goldberg is.

"Follow me," says Paez.

Paez leaves and the marines follow him. A medic comes up to our soldier.

"Are you alright?" he asks.

He sees he's bleeding on the shoulder. He sees the wine stained blood by his right ankle.

"Let me help you to the chopper," the medic says.

Our soldier struggles with him.

"You're not gonna take me alive," he says.

"Take it easy, Riley," says the medic reading his name tag. "I'm here to take you back to base. Get some medical attention."

Our soldier sees him jeering and laughing at him. Taunting him. "We'll capture you alive American swine." This is what he hears in his mind. This medic, he looks like a terrorist. Our soldier takes his Beretta from his holster and points it at the medic.

"Take it easy, friend," says the medic, "I'm here to help."

The chopper pilot is watching. He's on his radio. He grabs for his pistol, but he can't get a good shot at our soldier. The medic is in the way. The marines acknowledge. They're on their way back. Keep him occupied.

"You're not gonna take me alive, you fucking Arabs," says Riley.

He's waving the Beretta. He looks around. There are Arabs everywhere. They're pointing at him and laughing. They're coming to get him.

Our soldier puts the Beretta to his temple.

"You're not gonna take me alive you mother fuckers," he says.

They're gaining on him. The medic is yelling.

"Don't do it soldier, don't do it. We can get you help."

Our soldier is hearing something different.

"You'll tell us everything you American pig. We've got you now."

He pulls the trigger as the medic reaches for his hand. He's not fast enough. A spray of bloody mist erupts from the opposite side of our soldier's head. He falls like he's fallen into a hole.

"Noooo!" yells the medic.

The marines round the corner into the market. There's no one there. The medic is bending down at the body of our dead soldier. The pilot is climbing out of his chopper and running over. Our soldier's eyes are closed. There are no more voices, now. Everything is quiet. Everything is still. Everything is at peace.

My Son and I

He stands by the window. His once leathery face has been ground down by time into thin onion skin. His eyes are rheumy and watery. He looks far out into the distance. His vision is not as good as it once was, but his mind is sharp. Sharp as a tack, he'll tell you. He sees a car pull up. It's a fancy car and its owner takes real good care of it. A young man steps out from the front seat. He's tall, strong and handsome. He looks like a much younger version of the older man by the window.

The old man smiles.

"That's my son," he says, looking around, but no one else is there to hear him.

Still, he smiles alone, as his son walks up the long path to the main door. He sees his father through the glass window. The young man smiles and waves. You can tell it is a genuine smile. He shows teeth. Nice, white straight teeth. And there's warmth in it. You could warm yourself by the hearth of that smile. It beams out from his soul like hot coals.

The old man goes to the door and unlocks it. He opens it up. He is smiling too. Between the two of them they're having a smiling contest. The old man has been smiling longer, so he ought to win. But he doesn't. The young man has youth on his side, and adoration toward the old man, toward his father. So he wins. The young man wins. But you know, looking at them, you'd like to be either of them. A love like that, the warmth, it'll fill your heart to bursting.

"Hey, Dad," says the young man.

He bends down a little to embrace the old man. He hugs him tightly and holds on for dear life. You think that maybe they haven't seen each other for a long time. But the old man knows differently. He sees his son at least once a week. Oftentimes, more. They've always been close. Ever since the young man was a boy.

"Hello, my son," says the old man.

He embraces his son, and he feels the warm strength. He admires it in the young man. He used to enjoy such strength himself.

Though time is a thief, he takes with one hand, but he also gives with the other. The old man knows this. The years come along bearing their gifts. And he's grateful for them. But he can still admire the vigor of his young son.

"What would you like to do today?" asks the young man.

He releases his grip on the old man and they stand looking at each other. The younger man is a good two inches taller than the older man. The older man looks up at his son. Once, many years ago, it was the other way around. The young man, who was then a boy, looked up in awe and admiration at his father. Now the roles have reversed. The old man looks up at his son, if only a bit, and his eyes are filled with wonder at how good and honest and true the young man has become.

"I thought we could go for a walk in the park," the old man says.

"I'd like that, Dad," the son replies.

"Can I get you anything before we head out?" asks the old man.

The young man shakes his head. He has a crown of tightly curled hair. It is dark brown like the old man's was, many years ago. His mother loved it, God rest her soul. The old man only has wisps of what was once the same curly brown hair. He takes his thick meaty hand and rubs the palm of it across his thinning pate. He now has thin silver strands of hair covering his bald head. Covering age and liver spots. He blinks his watery eyes. He is filled to bursting with pride at his young son.

"Let's go Dad," says the young man.

The young man takes his father gently by the elbow and guides him cautiously down the path to the big, new, shiny car. He opens up the door for his father and helps the old man into the passenger seat. He closes the door softly behind him and walks around the front to the driver's door. He climbs in and looks over at his father.

"Buckle up for safety, Dad," he says.

The old man reaches with thick, sausage-like fingers that are as unwieldy as twigs. The arthritis is another gift that time has bequeathed him.

Many of the gifts are cruel and unkind. But some are treasures. Like the memories of his young son when he was just a boy. The old man remembers once when the young man was a boy playing in the beach sand in front of him. It seems so long ago and yet it feels like yesterday.

"Seat belt, Dad," says the young man again.

He has started the car but he is not driving it yet. He is looking over at the old man. His eyes are shining kindness and his tone is warm and gentle. The old man reaches for the seat belt, but the tendons and sinews of his arms and shoulder are like rusty cables. They tie his arms too close to his body. He can't reach across his chest for the seat belt. His sinews will not stretch that far. Time has clipped them like the wings of flightless doves. His fingers reach like worms for the seat belt and his joints ache. They are filled with sand and the sand grinds down daily at his knuckles and his bones. This is what it feels like.

"Here," says the young man, seeing his father struggle, "let me help you with that."

The young man reaches across the old man and pulls the seat belt across him.

The old man smells leather and wood and spice as the young man reaches across him. The young man wears the same cologne that the old man used to wear when he was younger.

He thinks back to those days. His son is on his lap. It is a Sunday morning and the father is reading to his son. It is a cowboy story. The son loved cowboy stories. Like the father, the son had a thirst for seeing good triumph over evil. And the cowboys were always good and the sheriff always won over the bank robbers and other ne'er-do-wells. The Lone Ranger was a favorite. But this story that the old man thinks about now, is a different story. A story about a loner, a loner who has to protect his family against horse rustlers.

The son wanted to become a cowboy when he was young. When he was eight years old, the father and the mother bought him a cowboy outfit for Christmas. Well, the son thought it was from Santa, but we now know better. It came with a six shooter and the boy would spend his days running around the house shooting all the bad guys. There were always bad guys, but the son always won.

And when the weather cleared up, when the snow had melted and the green buds burst upon the trees, the son would run around in the yard, climbing up and down trees and shooting all the bad guys. This went on for a few years.

And the son always knew that the Indians were never the bad guys. The father had told the son that. When he was young that the Indians were their friends, they were not the bad guys. This was what the father had told the son. And the son had believed it. The father had also instructed the son that Jews and blacks and Hispanics were all friends too. The only bad guys were those who hurt other people.

It was simple and easy and the son understood this naturally. The bad guys he spent his days shooting were horse rustlers and bank robbers, and sometimes, if he was really lucky, he would help capture train robbers. They were sneaky devils, the train robbers, but he caught a few now and then, and eventually he was made sheriff.

But over time, the childhood games of boys change into the characters of men. And the boy turned into a young man of great character.

This gave the old man the greatest joy.

"Okay, Dad, let's get going," says the young man.

The old man turns to him and smiles.

"Perhaps I can treat you to an ice cream. It seems like such a nice warm day today," says the old man wistfully.

"I'd like that, Dad," says the young man.

And the car starts to move slowly away from the house. This is the house where the young man grew up. Where the old man and his wife married and had a child. They only had the one child. This was not by choice; this was, in some ways, a gift of nature. The old man started his family when he was older. He was past forty. His wife, she was in her thirties. Between the two of them they lacked the potency to produce more than one child. And this was not without trying. They tried. It was fun, the trying, but it was futile.

Nevertheless, the old man and his wife never regretted only having one child. He was the apple of their eyes and they heaped their love upon him like the unending golden sands of time.

The three of them were happy for a very long time. But time can be a cruel bedfellow. The old man knows that. Time gives and he takes away. Sometimes he takes away more than he gives. And the old man has been robbed blind. But he is a good man and he dwells more on the gifts that have been given. The gifts that have been left. Like his son.

He looks over at the young man, driving the car. The young man is driving carefully, surely. He wants the ride to be pleasant for his old father. The father is after all, very old and fragile. But more than that, the father has heaped kindness upon the son all his life and the son will do the same for him, now. Now that the tables have turned. The young man has become the protector of the old. When before, it was the father who was protector of the son.

They drive down roads that they used to walk along when it was just the three of them. It was their routine that the father and the mother and the son would walk after dinner most nights, around the neighborhood. And it was a good neighborhood; there were many hardworking families here who made comfortable but honest livings.

The community was vibrant. It still is, but the old man remembers when it was a young community, newly built. Most of the families saw their children grow up here. They put their children through the same schools and they came to each other's birthday parties and bar mitzvahs. And over the years they got to know each other very well, and some of the children married each other. And sometimes these children, who grew up to be young men and young women, married someone of the same sex. And nobody got their nose out of joint, because it was love that moved this neighborhood, and it was love that the world always needed more of.

As the son now drives the father through the streets of their neighborhood, the father looks out of the window. The trees are now much bigger than when they first moved here. Like his son, the trees have grown up, big and strong. But still, there are young children playing in the front yards, skipping on sidewalks and jumping rope. The father can be seen smiling at them through the passenger window.

The father clutches at the seat belt and he pulls it gently away from him.

His hands are together as if he might be in prayer. But he is not in prayer, he is trying to loosen the seat belt. It feels tight around him. Unlike his son's embrace, this is not a warm embrace. And his lungs struggle against the seat belt. So he pulls it way from himself and it feels better.

They arrive at the park. The entrance way is a bit bumpy, it is a gravel road and the parking area is also sandy and gravely. The son finds a place under the canopy of a large tree. The tree is full of big, flat green leaves. Little mottled flashes of blue and white can be seen dancing between the leaves. The sky is the same blue as his son's first pajamas that the father can remember. And the smudges of white clouds are like his wife's makeup swabs.

The old man gives thanks for such a beautiful day. Though he does not know to whom or what he gives thanks. He used to believe in a God of some sort. Or he might even have called it a benevolent great spirit. But that was a long time ago. Now he just gives thanks. An open letter of thanks to whatever might be out there.

He's not sure why he gives thanks. But he knows that to give thanks is better than to dwell on the miseries. And time has taken much joy from the old man's life, and in its place it has left much misery. But the old man dwells on the small gifts that have been left behind. Like this moment with his son. It is a joy. A big bubble of joy that he can dwell in, far from the sharper memories. The memories that prick and cut and bleed.

The old man turns to look at his son, he prefers not to dwell in that thick tar of pain. His son is smiling. The young man always seems to have a smile. At least whenever he is with the old man. His son was in the Army. But that was a long time ago. Now he has his own consulting business. He's a military consultant he tells his father. The money is better, and he's tired of the blood and guts.

The young boy, who is now a young man, was a soldier. He fought hard for justice. He was one of the good guys. The old man knows this. He is proud of his son's service.

It was what young men who felt they could make a difference in the world did; help bring peace where there was war. Bring democracy where there was despotism.

The old man unbuckles the seat belt. His son is already out of the car and he is walking around the back towards the passenger door. He opens the passenger door and helps his father out of the car. The old man is old. He is a nonagenarian. He likes that word. It was a word his son taught him when he turned ninety. That was a few years ago. The old man is counting his blessings again. He can fit them in one hand. But it is enough. When he counts the blessings he does not feel the weight on his shoulders. That weight is the baggage of miseries that time has loaded upon his frail shoulders. This is what makes the old man bowed. The weight of loss and sadness and misery.

But then he looks down at his open palm. He has five fingers. Well, he knows there are only four fingers and a thumb.

But it is easy to call them five fingers. And these are the ways he counts his blessings. He folds his thumb into his palm. This is the first blessing. And this blessing is the young man who is with him today. The young man who comes to visit him at least once a week, though oftentimes more than that.

The young man is helping the old man out of the car. He takes the old man's hand in his and helps him out. Though the man is old, he is still spritely for his age. He is agile and he is thin. But he is healthy.

The old man is standing by the side of the car and he folds his index finger into his palm. This is blessing number two. Blessing number two is that he had a wonderful wife. A woman whom he loved more than life itself. In fact, in moments of weakness, when you listen to the man's thoughts when he is quiet and alone, you will know that he wished he could have taken her place. But death is choosey, and he takes the best ones for himself. And she was one of the best.

The years of pain that he now carries, they do not undo the blessing that was the time he had with her.

The first years were terribly hard. He knows that. The days came and with them the painful lashings. Each day, they opened up old wounds and cut fresh ones into him. But time gives gifts, and one of those was the salve of time that healed the worst of the wounds. And his son was with him. A growing boy, a bright boy who hurt, too, and with whom he shared the sorrows.

But this index finger that is tucked now into his palm, this is the blessing of his wife. And he looks up at his son, and he sees her face in his. He is his mother's son and the old man is grateful.

"What a wonderful day, Dad," says the son. "Can you hear the birds chirping?"

And the young man looks up at the canopy of trees and he points to a bird.

"See the Mockingbird, Dad. The chirping, whistling. Isn't it lovely?" he asks.

The old man smiles and tilts his head upwards. His watery eyes see the gray Mockingbird. He admires its smart dress and whistling tune.

The young man has always admired birds.

At one time when he was a boy, after he had outgrown his adventures of being a cowboy, he thought of exploring the world as an airline pilot. And he did. He got his pilot's license with the Army. He was lucky enough to fly both airplanes and helicopters, though he mostly flew Apaches.

In his bedroom the old man still has a picture of his young son in front of his Apache. It was the first Apache he flew, and the photograph was of his first sortie. The old man never served his country in the military, but he admired the men and women who did. And he was most proud of his son's service.

"What a wonderful sound, son," says the old man. "Where did you learn all about the different bird calls?"

They start walking towards the paved path just off the dusty parking lot. The old man shivers. He is cold, though he is not sure why, the sun is shining brightly and the sky is blue. There is hardly a breeze in the air.

"Well, you know Dad, that ever since I was young I've admired birds and their ability to fly.

That's why I became a pilot in the Army. Anyway, I've spent so much time outdoors when I could, just watching and listening and learning about the different bird calls of the songbirds wherever I've been."

The old man is listening and nodding his head. He walks slowly. Slower than the young man would like. But the young man is patient with his father. And so they walk as fast as the slowest of them. And the slowest of them is the old man.

The old man looks at his palm again. He folds his middle finger into his palm, over the thumb. This is his third blessing. He remembers the first two. He is blessed for his son in his life and he is blessed for his wife. His third blessing is for this day. A beautiful day like this one is a gift. He catches a whiff of the scent of wildflowers, it is sweet and spicy. A corner of this scent reminds him of the smell of his late wife. He sees her now as though it were yesterday. She is laughing. He is teasing her just before they are heading out for a show.

He tries to remember what the show was. It is hard.

There are many memories in his mind that blow around like sheets of paper. It is hard to capture just one to see it more closely. But this is his third blessing. This day. This day filled with the drapes of a blue sky, mottled with white swatches of clouds. The lovely sound of songbirds singing and the warmth of the sun on his face. The old man stops for a moment and turns to face the sun. He looks up towards it, closing his eyes. He feels the warmth of it on his thin skin. It is a liquid warmth. Like warm oil. He breathes deeply. Life smells good.

"If we're lucky enough, we might get to hear some more songbirds on our walk today," says the young man. "There aren't many people around, which is a good thing. More songbirds might be out and closer to the edge of the path."

"I'd like that, son," says the old man. "Please point them out to me."

And the old man turns and opens his eyes and looks at his son. His son is beaming at him, like the sun was just now. There is still the joy and boyish wonder in his son's face at the brightness and bountifulness of life.

The old man hopes he never loses that love for life.

"Always remain in awe," the old man says to his son.

The son looks at him and smiles.

"You taught me, Dad," he says. "There is so much beauty and grandeur and wonder on this planet. How can one not be in awe?"

The old man smiles and they walk on again. They are on the paved path now. On both sides of them the brush and wildlife of flora is thick and vivid. It reaches up to mid-thigh. Nature is in the throes of ecstatic growth. The colors are brilliant and they pour into the eyes deeply. Nature is putting on a show. There are blues and reds, oranges, and glaring greens. It is more intense than a painting. The old man is in awe, too. He bows down towards a red flower in reverence and sniffs at the petals.

It smells like a rose but it is not a rose. It has another name. This scent even more strongly reminds him of his wife. Yes, he remembers, now.

They were going out on their anniversary. It was their twelfth wedding anniversary.

The sitter had arrived to watch over their son. He would have been twelve. His wife loved live theater. They were going for an early dinner at a wonderful restaurant. He remembers it now, the restaurant was called "Cutting Board" and the theater was going to show "A Dream of Sorrows."

He remembers it now, his wife loved the theater. There is a twinge in his heart. A lump in his throat, this squeezing, another helping of lashings. They never got to the theater. A drunkard ran them down as they were crossing the road from the parking lot. She was looking at him with a big smile on her face, her arm tucked into his elbow and her shawl over her neck. That's when it happened. He only found out she was dead days later, when he came out of the coma. He wished he hadn't. A tear drops from his eye and bursts on the red petal.

The young man lays a warm, comforting arm over his shoulder.

"Are you okay, Dad?" he asks.

The old man gets up and looks at his son. He blinks his eyes shut tight, and tears trickle down his cheek.

The young man reaches into his pocket and takes his handkerchief and dabs away the tears.

"I miss your mother," says the old man, "I don't want anything to ever happen to you."

The young man looks down at his father. He smiles comfortingly.

"I miss her, too. But don't worry about me, Dad, I am safe. Nothing can happen to me."

The old man tries on a brave smile, but it does not fit naturally on his face. He lets it fall off and they walk on, enjoying each other's company. They pass by a young woman jogging in tight black yoga pants. She wears a blue strapless shirt. Her pony tail flicks from one side to the other, like it is swatting flies. She is not wearing makeup and still she is attractive. She smiles at the two of them as she jogs on by. Though in truth, the smile is more for the young man.

The old man looks at his son, but he is deep in thought. He has his hands in his pocket and he does not see the woman go by. The old man wonders if his son will ever marry. If he will ever get a grandchild before he dies.

"I think she liked you," says the old man.

The young man looks up and smiles.

"What...oh, yeah. Was she nice?" he asks.

"I think she was. She smiled at you, but you didn't see her."

The young man shakes his head.

"No, I didn't, I was deep in thought," he says.

"When will you get married?" asks the old man.

The son is again looking down at the gray pavement of the path they are walking on. He shrugs his shoulders. Strong, muscled shoulders. Even though he is no longer in the Army, the young man still takes care of his body.

"I don't know, Dad, I guess I just haven't found the right one," answers the son.

"I really liked that young lady you brought round the house a few times. What was her name again?"

"Rebecca?" asks the son.

The old man shakes his head; that was not her name. Still, these memories like paper get shuffled and blown about by the wind of time in his mind. What was her name, again.

"Veronica, I think," says the old man. "I think her name was Veronica."

The son looks up at his father and smiles. He shakes his head slowly.

"No, I never dated a Veronica, I think you're thinking of Vivian. Goodness, that was eons ago."

The old man nods.

"Yes, that's right, Vivian. Whatever happened to her?"

They walk on for a bit in silence. The young man is deep in thought. Finally he stops walking and the old man stops next to him. He turns to look at his father.

"She cheated on me, Dad, didn't you know that? I told Mom, I'm sure she would have told you."

The old man is searching frantically in the old dusty cabinets of his mind. There are so many memories strewn about like papers blown about in a storm. He can't remember this bit of information his son has told him. But he can't tell him he doesn't.

"Yes, yes, I remember now, your mother did tell me. I'm sorry she did that son, you deserve better."

The young man smiles at his father and puts his arm around his shoulder as they take off walking down the path again.

"That's pretty much what Mom said. I guess I just haven't found anyone better yet," says the son.

"You will," says the old man, and he believes it.

And you would believe it too. You can look at the young man and know that he is much sought after by women. He is handsome and tall and good natured. He is popular amongst his peer group, too. He has more male friends than he can spend time with.

The old man smiles with this knowledge. He is the lucky one. He gets to enjoy his son's company at least once a week, oftentimes more.

They walk on and the bird songs change. The old man hears a new call from a different bird. It is a single squawk. He listens again, it happens again. The squawks are a few seconds apart.

"Which bird makes that song?" he asks his son.

They stop and the son listens. He looks over to a clump of trees off the side of the path a few feet. The young man pushes his ear towards the trees to listen. The single squawk happens. He hears it. He waits for it again. A few seconds later it happens again, and then again. He looks more earnestly towards the trees. He sees the bird. He points his finger towards it.

"It's a Blue Jay, Dad, just like your favorite baseball team," the young man says. "Do you see it?"

The old man looks up to the trees. He is too far away for his eyes to see the bird. This is what the thief, time, has taken from him. He used to be able to see things far away. Crystal clear his vision was. But time has stolen that from him. Now he looks at life through gauze, muslin. Everything tinged with haze and smoke. The smoke of time has tainted his looking lenses, his eyes. But he nods. He remembers what the Blue Jay looks like.

"Up there, the second tallest tree, about two thirds of the way up. You can see him, can't you, Dad? Such beautiful vibrant blue feathers," says the young man.

The old man nods again.

"Yes, I see him," he lies.

He doesn't like to lie to his son. But these are small white lies. They die quickly and no one is the worse for it.

"Gorgeous colors. Just like that first Blue Jay we saw when you were ten years old. Do you remember that? We were out walking like we are now. But it was a nature trail. And we saw a few of them. Remember?"

The young man has brought his hand down. He's still looking at the trees, watching and listening to the Blue Jay. He smiles broadly. He's showing his teeth again. A warm smile. Bright and warm as this day.

"Of course I remember, Dad," the son says. "How could I not? The Blue Jay is my favorite bird. Ever since I knew its name was the same as your favorite baseball team. Remember when we watched the Blue Jays win the World Series in thirty-six."

"I think it was thirty-nine, son," says the old man. "Thirty-six was when your mother died.

But I do remember that. It was a happy moment for us, wasn't it?"

And the old man puts his hand on his son's shoulder. It is an old hand. A hand that looks like the bark of a tree. A fragile tree. The veins are dark and sullen and his fingers are gnarled and bent like they shouldn't be.

These are the things that time steals. The memories are there. He can remember the Blue Jay he first saw with his son when his son was ten years old. But this new Blue Jay, he can not see it very well. It is too small to be seen through the muslin over his eyes.

The old man takes his hand off his son's shoulder. He puts his ring finger down into his palm. He is counting his blessings again. There is no use counting the miseries. He could spend the rest of his days counting that way and never be finished. It is always better to focus on something to be grateful for, rather than commiserating with misery. That's what he told his son when his wife, his son's mother, died. He needs to lead by example. Even after all these years he must still lead by example.

His ring finger is bent in towards his palm and this is his fourth blessing. Remember, he can count his blessings on one hand. This fourth blessing is that he is still alive. Yes, you might say it is a double edged sword. This blessing that time has given him extra life. He has long ago said goodbye to old friends. He has no one left now but his son. His wife is gone, as are his brother and his sisters. The nieces and nephews do not come by to visit; neither do the grandnieces and grandnephews. But he does not mind that. He has his son who visits him at least weekly.

And he will let time visit him and take much from him, even when the only thing time leaves him with is extra days. Because days like this make it worth living. The shoulders may sag from the weight of miseries, but these days, these bright sunny days, make the journey worth taking.

Time takes with the one hand, but what he gives with the other can make it all worth while. If you have the right attitude. If you're willing to look the other way. The way where the gifts are.

Precious moments and time with loved ones. This is why life is worth living.

The next day could be a good one. The next day is always a new chance. A chance you might do better, be better and make things right.

They walk on, the young man and the old man. Shoulder to shoulder, their steps are not quite in rhythm. The old man shuffles his feet. His walking feet are heavy. He has many miles on them. The young man is prone to walk swiftly, but he does not. He walks with his father. Slowly, carefully, methodically, as if walking was an act that had to be done with much planning and forethought. The old man walks like a wise and old Zen Buddhist monk.

He is deliberate. You might mistake him for conducting a walking meditation. And he does meditate, in a manner of speaking. He walks thoughtfully, his mind full of thoughts. These papers that are shuffled in his mind by the winds of time.

The old man stretches out his fingers, and he counts them. One, two, three and four blessings. He knows there is a fifth blessing that he is grateful for. It hangs and lingers on his small finger.

But he cannot recollect it now.

So he walks, looking at the ground, and then at his son, who walks next to him. They walk as one, but their feet do not match. The old man has smaller feet and he takes smaller steps.

"How about that ice cream you promised?" asks the son as they walk by the ice cream stand in the park.

The old man stops and walks over to the vendor.

"Two popsicles," he asks.

"My favorite," says the son. "You remembered."

The old man fishes out some coins from his pocket. Not quite thirty pieces of silver, but somehow he feels a little bit like a traitor. He does not know where this feeling comes from. He looks at his son. The son he loves more than life itself. He does not feel he betrayed him. Perhaps he feels he betrayed his wife. But that cannot be true, either. He lived with integrity and honor. This he taught to his son. And his son is a man of honor and integrity. He fights for what is right and just and good in this world. Like the old man does in his small corner of this life.

The old man accepts the popsicles from the vendor and he hands one to his son. His son is smiling big and wide as the horizon. The old man smiles too. They unwrap their popsicles. The young man takes a lick of his first and shivers. It is cold and tart.

"So good, Dad, thanks," he says.

The old man tastes his. He shivers. It is cold; it is chilling him to the very bones. He looks at his son with his rheumy, droopy eyes. Sadness mists them up.

"You know I love you, son, don't you?" he asks.

He is asking earnestly. The old man wants to be sure. He must know that the son knows he loves him. The young man nods.

"Every time we spoke, Dad. You always told me you loved me. I always knew it, I always felt it."

A tear, like a clear snake slithers down his cheeks. The old man blinks and he shivers. The ice cream is making him feel much colder.

"Don't cry, Dad. You know I love you, too."

The old man drips more tears down his cheek.

They fall like beginning rain to the pavement. The old man nods. He opens his mouth to speak, and his voice is cracked. His lips quiver. Not because he is cold, but because he is sad.

"I know," the old man says, "I just wish we had more time."

The day is still bright and sunny, and his son stands in front of him, licking his popsicle, just like he did when he was eight years old and it was the first popsicle he ever had.

"We have right now, Dad," says the son, wise beyond his years. "Right now is all we've ever had."

Something is touching the old man on the shoulder. It is squeezing him and shaking him gently. He looks at his son, but it is not his son.

"Mr. Daedalus..."

The old man looks around. Before him things are changing. He cannot see his son anymore. He is once again alone. He looks down and his feet are covered in a blanket of wet, white snow.

He can see his slippers on his feet. He looks at his chest and sees the soft blue robe that he is wearing.

It is dotted with melting white stars of snow. He looks up at the hand that is on his shoulder. It is a woman's hand.

"Mr. Daedalus, come, we must get you inside. You'll catch a terrible cold. We've been looking all over for you. You'll get us all in heaps of trouble."

The old man looks at the young woman and smiles. She is smiling at him. She is young and fit and she reminds him of his late wife.

"Penelope," the old man says.

The young woman wipes away the blanket of white snow that has crowned the old man's balding head. The old man is shaking. It is cold outside. The middle of winter. The young woman shakes her head and smiles at him.

"No, Mr. Daedalus, I am Rebecca. What are we going to do with you? You know you're not allowed outside in the middle of winter, by yourself."

This young woman takes the old man by the crook of the elbow and leads him up the path towards the house. The old man shuffles alongside her. He looks at the big white building with many windows and many lights on in the windows.

"I was visiting my son," he says to her. "He came to visit me and we had ice cream together."

The young woman looks at him with kindness in her eyes. She stays close by his side as she helps him up towards the residence.

"Your son died serving his country over forty years ago, Mr. Daedalus. He died in The Unending War. He was a very brave pilot. See, he got the Purple Heart that you still have around your neck."

She reaches over and touches the purple satin ribbon that is around the old man's neck. The old man feels the weight of the medal thumping softly against his heart. Like his son's heartbeat when he held him close to his chest when he was a young boy. The old man sees the boy's face. It is smiling at him as he picks him up and hugs him close. He kisses the boy on the forehead.

Time has taken so much. The lashings come again. He remembers the news. The two smart Army men standing at his door. One was a colonel. They wore grim faces.

They had bad news. The worst news he had ever received since his wife's death.

He remembers the white gloves offering the flag so neatly folded. Still, the red stripes visible, the blood stolen from him.

"Come on, Mr. Daedalus, let's get you inside and I'll make you a nice hot cocoa and you can tell me all about your son."

And the old man looks at his hand. His palm is facing up, and he tucks his thumb and then his index finger into his palm. He tucks in his middle finger and his ring finger. Then he tucks in his small finger.

He remembers now, the fifth blessing. This one he calls the kindness of strangers. It was strangers who offered him the lifeline to carry on when everything had been taken away. And it is, even now, strangers who help him carry on.

Forever Famine

It was during the Forever Famine that I saw my pa kill a man. But that happens later than where I'm at right now. I want to tell the story from the beginning. Because me saying my pa killed a man makes you think he's a murderer. And he's not, see. I mean, he killed a man, I ain't arguing that, and yeah, it was in cold blood. But you see, it wasn't like that. He was protecting his family. Me and ma.

You've gotta understand the Forever Famine before you can pass judgment 'kay? You ain't know hunger unless you also knew the Forever Famine. Those of you who lived through it, you all understand. You know what it was like. Some of us tried to make porridge with crushed bones and sand. It wasn't good. You don't need me telling you that. You can figure it out yourself. But that's what we tried.

Powdered dried bones. And I'm not saying these were just animal bones, neither. No, we didn't have the luxury of being choosy. "Choosy," that's what my pa said.

"You can't be choosy, son," he said, "not during these times. These hungry times."

He was right, but he was also wrong. Lots of folks were choosy. We had hundreds of them. The Choosy Ones, we called them. And it wasn't a compliment, neither. No, siree. It was an insult. But they took it like a compliment. Maybe it was the hunger. It makes you feel some kind of crazy. The mind goes woozy, too.

But I'll talk about the Choosy Ones in good time. But you have to understand. Life was cheap. Helluva cheap. In some places, and I'm not saying this happened around these parts, but you could buy human meat. I know that sounds gross now, and it is. Heck, it was gross even then. But nobody told you about it. It ain't like you could go to your local butcher and ask for a nice human butt. No, siree, but some places, like in dark alleys and faraway fields folks would set up shop for a few hours. And if you were quick, they'd sell you a steak or something like that. Only it wasn't steak. At least not from a cow, you know.

No, siree. I don't mean to upset you. Animal flesh was expensive, only the rich could get some. And it was rare too. Not how it was cooked. No, siree, how much of it there was. It cost more per ounce than the equivalent in gold. I ain't kidding 'bout that. That's the God's honest truth.

Not that it means much. God's truth. I mean, God died during the Forever Famine. Let me get back to that for a minute. The Forever Famine lasted fourteen years. The scientists figure we lost just about ninety percent of everything.

Really. I mean I'm talking about everything. Well, everything that lived. Us, the humans, didn't quite lose ninety percent. We lost over eight billion souls. That's what they said after the Forever Famine finished. We lost eight billion of the almost nine billion souls. Funny thing is though, if you have a soul, doesn't that mean there's some kinda spirit or God out there?

But there wasn't during the Forever Famine. I mean really, there wasn't. The things people did. The depths of depravity.

Even now, just thinking about that, I sometimes lose my appetite. And that's funny, 'cos the hunger is never gone, not for those of us who made it through. We're always hungry, and now we're fat, 'cos we can't stop eating. I mean, like I said, I sometimes lose my appetite, but I'm always hungry. I'm always eating.

And there's food now. A lot of it. That's all we do. We make and eat things. Anything. It's sad and gross really, but that's how it is. So I was saying how we lost everything. Or about ninety percent of everything. Anything that lived. We lost ninety percent of plants that grow, flowers. If it could be eaten, we ate it until there was none left. If it couldn't be eaten, we killed it to make room for things we could eat.

And we know how it happened, this Forever Famine. It happened because of them. The Shark Faces we call them. The bankers and businessmen who just lusted after power and hunger and couldn't stop themselves.

They ate up the world and spat out the bones for us to chew on.

Yes, siree. They vomited all over the land with their chemicals and mass weapons of agricide. That's a word I learnt during the Forever Famine.

These men did nothing for us, but poison us. That's the truth. God's honest truth. But like I said, God ain't around no more. But still, it's funny the things that stick around with us. Us being small and all, needing something bigger to believe in.

We lost belief during the Forever Famine. We lost hope. We lost our belief in capitalism. We lost our belief in Mother Nature. We lost hope in each other. You wouldn't know the kinda world we lived in back then. It's only been three good years since the end of the Forever Famine. And folks are still worried. Three harvests, and we're stuffing ourselves. And still the gaps won't heal. We can't find a place of comfort, yet. But I reckon it's coming, otherwise I wouldn't be telling you this story.

It's kind of a confession. A sorta white flag. A flickering flame of hope if you'd like to call it that.

If you're interested in me, I can tell you a little about me.

It don't matter, it'll probably be a long time before you get this. Those of us who grew up during the Forever Famine, and I'm one of them, are small. Most of the men don't hit five feet six and most women don't make it to five feet even. Hunger eats you up. Robs you of your future. Maybe you know that.

I'm one of the lucky ones, 'cos we weren't choosy. No, siree. Like my pa said, we ate what we could. We ate anything we could. Including the man my pa shot and killed. Yeah, I'm sick about it now. I truly am, but you've gotta understand what it was like. And I'm gonna tell you. If you'll stick around a bit with me, I'll tell you all about it.

I'm one of the lucky ones, like I said. I'm five feet five. But here's the kicker, I now weigh 225 pounds. I'm fat. I told you, we just can't stop eating. And now that the hunger didn't kill us, it looks like the food will do us in.

Ironic isn't it? We can last through fourteen years of the Forever Famine and in probably under five years, most of us will eat ourselves to death.

I was five when it started. And it started quick. One fall we had plenty to eat. I was out with my parents on Halloween trick or treating. The next fall, my pa and ma were out scrounging for food. Stripping bark off trees and trying to make soup with twigs and leaves.

It's not funny. You'll be surprised what you'd eat when you've been starving for weeks. Like for instance, I remember when I would keep a small pebble in my mouth pretty much all day. Just to have something in there. Something for my saliva to work with. After years like that, this pebble is smooth as glass. It's been polished to a mirror like finish, smooth and black. Black as the night sky. That's what your tongue and palette and teeth can do. And it helps. It's something to keep the worst of the hunger away.

I was five, like I said, at the start of the Forever Famine and I didn't understand what it meant. The first five years of my life I'd been well nourished.

My folks had taken care of me. Pa always had the biggest, fattest cuts, but ma made sure I didn't do without, neither. No, siree, she was good that way. God bless her soul.

She's dead now, and I don't believe she's with God, 'cos like I said, God died in that Forever Famine. Ask anyone. Priests became beggars, and they ate the body of Christ. Literally, like I was telling you, there were occasions when we ate each other. The priests were used to it. You know, eating that wafer that they said literally became the body of Christ.

I saw one priest, once, cross himself as he gnawed at a bone. It was a forearm bone, an ulna I think they calls it. Had a little gristle on it, not much meat. See, the folks that died first, they was the weak ones. The ones that wasted away easier than most. Soon the authorities clamped down and threw people in jail to die if they was caught eating meat. People meat that is.

This is not meant to be a horror story, okay. No, siree, these are just the facts 'kay. It's not even a zombie story. Zombies aren't real, we all know that. But this is real, and people ate people. Not all of us. Not the Choosy Ones, like I told you. But some of us did. Yeah, I did too. I'm sorry about it. But I'm trying to get you to understand.

Call it a warning, if you will. The way we're feasting all the time now. The way we's getting fat. The ways folks are reproducing like rabbits. Not that there's any rabbits left. They're long gone extinct. They was the first to go. Amongst the first.

And I hear what you're thinking. You're thinking, hell, rabbits reproduce a lot right? Yeah, so? And when you've got nothing to eat, and you've got nothing to give the rabbits to eat, then what? They die. You eat them, and you can wait, but when they're starving they ain't reproducing. No, siree. That's the God's honest truth.

I was saying how we ain't zombies. But folks back then looked like zombies I guess. I told you the mind makes you woozy when you're starving.

And folks you'd see had sunken in eyes and cheeks. Lots of them had tooths missing and cracked lips that wouldn't stop bleeding. And their eyes were just dark as coal, and the sockets too, like the gray ash after a fire.

But these are real people I'm talking about here. This is what happened to my ma before she left. And when I say left, I mean when she left us for the ground. We didn't eat her, I couldn't, she left us for the ground same time pa did. But other folks ate them. I could tell, you'll see.

But I remember my pa saying "It ain't natural, son, to eat kin." By then we'd eaten people meat, but when my ma n' pa left for the ground I didn't, not even one time thinks of eating them. And not just 'cos I was scared neither.

And that's what them Choosy Ones said.

"People meat is just the same as other meat," they said. "And we won't eat meat."

The Choosy Ones. Funny thing is, they was right. Yes, siree. You see, we don't eat no meat anymore. Can't, that's why.

We literally can't, you see, we're barely producing enough crops on vulnerable land. We can't afford to give it to some animal to eat. It's too intensive, they said. They told us these things way back before the Forever Famine.

But those Shark Faces, they said not to worry. Science will save us. Well, science died during the Forever Famine. At least our blind belief in science. God and science, both dead. So what do we believe in now? Nothing. We believe in this day. This one day.

There are no tomorrows. Tomorrows are sorrows. This day, this one day is our bread. Daily bread you know, literally. Just this day. When I put myself to sleep at night, I don't think about tomorrows, tomorrows are sorrows. If I wake at daybreak, then that's the day I believe in.

I can't count the number of times my pa would put me to bed at night and tell me the same thing.

"Rest eternal, son," he said. It was almost like a prayer, like he wished me to bed so that I might die. And that's not unkind. I don't hate my father for it. Most nights that was my prayer too.

I'd stick my twig like fingers together and asked to die. Plead really. Well, at least I did before God died. That happened on the third year of our Forever Famine. By that time we'd lost fifty percent of humanity. Almost five billion people.

I don't know if you can imagine that. But try this. Let's pretend you and your wife have two kids. Out of the four of you, who do you wish dead? And wishing them dead is a kindness. The Forever Famine was a nightmare, a living hell. Yes, siree. You can believe that.

We used to envy the dead. They'd lost their humanity for sure, but so had we. We were the living dead. Kinda like zombies I guess, only this was real. Nobody trusted no one no more. The authorities were corrupt. Squads of goons once called police would roam the streets and they'd just come into your house and if you had something to eat, they'd just take it from you.

Why I say it was the third year of the Forever Famine that God died was because that's when guns and ammunition and stuff like that became illegal.

You couldn't buy the stuff anymore. No, siree. You actually had to hand it in to the government.

Hah, that's funny. Nobody did. So it became us versus them and us versus each other. The hunger made you do crazy stuff. It was the hunger in part that made my pa kill that man. Maybe I should be more honest. He killed a policeman. But don't get all high 'n' mighty. This wasn't a good policeman. There weren't anymore good guys then. Just shades of bad guys.

I'll get to that. It's worth the telling. But I want to tell you about the second year. It was a bounty and a curse. I was six then, remember? I was thin as a rail. But you've probably got the wrong impression of me. You're probably thinking I'm stick thin with a big belly. You're thinking kwashiorkor. Like those images of those kids in Africa, a long, long time ago.

What most of us older kids had can best be described as marasmus. Kwashiorkor is more common in young kids, just weaned who suffer protein deficiency more so than calorie deficiency.

Marasmus is just severe deficiency of everything, protein, carbohydrates and fat. I learned this. Being hungry you learn stuff, you find books and you eat them. Sometimes you read 'em first too. I read about that kwashiorkor stuff and the marasmus. Sounds like an old man I read about once in relation to the Bible. Erasmus I think was his name. Somehow related to the Bible, or religion or something. But that's not important.

So, I was six years old, rail thin. You could play the xylophone on my ribs. I was so thin that if you turned me sideways in the wind, the air would make a whistling sound passing over me like you can do with a piece of paper.

That last bits a joke. I can look back now and joke about it, even if I am eating myself to death now.

But this ain't about me now. No, siree. This is about how it was. And I was six years old. A sullen and sick child. I had a cough and runny nose all the time. I had long learnt to stop complaining about the hunger. Most of the time I was outside trying to find food. And by that time, it was getting real hard to find anything worth eating.

We lived in the suburbs then. Working class it used to be. But there was nothing living no more. Not much anyway. I'd look out my back yard and all I'd see was nothing. Ground, dirt, nothing. No living thing. Half the houses empty, right? By this time we're half dead. Remember, I told you. Half of humans is gone.

Ninety percent of anything living is gone. So you're thinking why not eat the other ten percent. That ten percent has packed up its bags and moved. That ten percent is living where humans can't go.

I mean, sometimes, I'd find a tasty morsel. Maybe a cockroach. That was like Thanksgiving. I never told my ma and pa about it. No, siree, them insects were treats for me. When I could find them. Ants too. They're bitter, worse than lemons. But you do it. You eat them, 'cos the hunger controls you.

God's honest truth, you're like a puppet. Hunger is dangling you from strings. You do what it tells. And it tells you weird things. Like how good them people look to eat. That's what made us into zombies.

Not real zombies, that's just stories, I mean like real people eating other people. That's where I'm getting with this. I was six. You gotta remember that. A small boy, rail thin. My mother was alive then still. That was before she left us for the ground.

I'd met the Choosy Ones by then. I didn't get it. These were people what used to be called vegetarians and something else, vegans or something. Them wouldn't eat nothing that lived or moved. I think that's right.

Anyway, they talked all the time. On the sides of the streets, they'd bend your ear, tell you that we shouldn't be eaten meat, shouldn't have done it. How that's what got us here in the first place.

I get it now. I didn't get it then. Eventually the Choosy Ones landed up in jail. For their own protection. Some of that was true, folks wanted to kill 'em and eat 'em. Mostly because they were annoying. But still, not all the Choosy Ones were vegetarian, some of them figured it was wrong to eat people meat. They was right too.

But you gots to understand the hunger. The Forever Famine gave you the hunger and hunger made you do crazy things. That's the God's honest truth. So, as I was saying about my pa. I want to tell it like it happened. It's important like that, see?

I come home one day from looking around the neighborhood for something to eat. I found a small little weed. It was horrible, tasted like acid, but I ate it. It kept the hunger away for a minute.

So I come home and pa is all smiles, so is ma. I hadn't seen smiles for months then. Many months, maybe over a year. Hard to tell. So I asks my pa what's going on. I'm only little, right? You get that, six years old.

Pa says to me, he says "I got potatoes son, I got them goddamn potatoes."

I didn't know what potatoes was, then. I had forgotten. I hadn't seen potatoes in over a year. And when you're young, you forget stuff like that. So, my pa, he shows me. He opens his big hands. Bony hands but they're big and I count six potatoes. They look like big fat worms.

I remember opening my mouth in awe. And my drool dribbles down my chin. My ma wipes it away with her apron. She says to me we're gonna cook two of 'em and plant the rest for next year. I don't understand that. I mean a bird in the hand right. I wanted to eat them all. Right then.

It's late winter, and the cold is always there. It's like the bully that's always with you. The cold was my worst fear. I was cold all the time. 'Cept in summer. On a hot summer day I could feel warm. But most times, I'm cold. But I don't shake no more. Nobody shakes anymore. You've got no energy to spare so the body gives up shaking.

You just live next to cold and it eats you. Like the hunger. Theys like two wolves eating at you. The cold nibbles at you until you're weak and then hunger finishes you off. I've seen it plenty of times. Makes me sick just thinking 'bout it. I'm shaking now, like I'm cold, but I'm not cold no more.

So my father goes into the yard that night, when it's dark. My mother comes out with him and I go out, too.

We don't use no light. We don't want the neighbors to know. We don't have neighbors right or left, but folks are out scrounging all the time so you gots to be careful. The moon is half full and my pa digs in the ground with a fork from the kitchen. We didn't have no shovels then, we gave them up for food the year before. We gave up everything we didn't need for food.

We don't have anything now but the essentials. Forks and knives, guns n' ammo. My pa cuts each potato into a whole bunch of little pieces. He tells me it's all in the eyes. I don't know what he means.

He says to me. "Each eye will give us lots of potatoes. We'll eat 'til we're full, son, next summer."

He puts each piece in its own hole and he lets me cover it up with the dirt and pat it down good with my shoes. Dozens of holes for lots of potatoes. I start dreaming right then that I'll be fat next summer.

"These will bring us dozens of potatoes," my pa says. And he takes his hands and he makes them into a big hill.

"We'll get these many," he says and I can see them all filling this hill he's creating with his arms.

And we go inside and my ma boils the potatoes. I'm salivating the whole time. The smell makes me nervous, it's so powerful I'm scared people will smell it miles away and come rob us before we can eat 'em.

But it doesn't happen. Even in the Forever Famine, sometimes you get lucky. My pa tells my ma he stole these seed potatoes from the seed store in town. It was already ransacked, but in the back was them seed potatoes, just these six he says. They were in the corner out of sight.

"We'll eat like royalty," pa says to ma and me while he holds his potato with his one hand and bites it. Ma and me share the other one. I've never tasted anything so good. No, siree. I still can't remember tasting anything so good.

And through those early months of the waiting for them potatoes, just the thought feeds us. It's enough that we can hope. But in July I can tell my pa is worried. I can see it in his bulging eyes and the whispers he says to ma.

"I don't know how to hide the leaves and stalks," he says to ma. He's real nervous. He oils his shotgun constantly and he speaks to himself. He says how he'll kill anyone who tries to take his potatoes.

Ma looks at me and gives me a smile. Says there's nothing to worry about, we'll be eating like royalty soon. Already we've taken a couple of stalks up from the ground. They give us good potatoes. They're only small, but I get four to myself. I never been so full in a long while.

We're staring at the third year of the Forever Famine. We can tell it by the harvests we miss. Each summer is another year in the Forever Famine. I'm hearing that we gone lost eighty percent of people by this time.

And when I go out into the yard I see why pa's scared. I'm scared, too. I never seen so much greenery in years. It's like a big beacon. I feel like everyone can see it.

And pa and ma is trying to hide it. They build makeshift sloping walls to lean in to it. But you gots to keep the tops open for them potatoes to see the sun so they can grow good.

And pa tries to cover these lean-tos with mud and dirt and it works pretty well. But he and ma is not sleeping together. He's up sitting outside watching the potatoes with his shotgun by his side like ol' Rustler used to sit by him. Rustler was our lab. 'Til he died.

He died of starvation. We couldn't feed him. All the food we gots then, we had to eat it. And he died hungry. I remember him looking at us at the table one time, his big ol' eyes sad. He was whimpering, and I gave him a small crust from my bread.

Pa smacked me upside the head then. It hurt, but not as much as seeing Rustler die. But we didn't kill him. No, siree, we're not like that. Some folks killed their pets and ate 'em. Not us. I mean we ate Rustler, but only after he had died natural first.

And that was the hardest thing I ever done. Ma cooked him up in a big soup an we ate him for a few days. I cried every time I ate him. The tears splashing in my bowl like seasoning. Pa didn't say nothing.

Ma looked like she might cry, too. But she didn't. But every meal I cried. I kept seeing him looking at me like he did that one time.

And even now I wake up crying in the middle of the night from nightmares about that. Rustler was the last dog I ever saw in my life. Matter of fact, he was the last animal I reckon I ever did see. For real, I'm not talking like in the pictures.

And the Choosy Ones, after I ate my dog, I got to understand them better. I mean, I eaten a man too, and there ain't much difference in eating a cow or a pig or a dog or a man. So them Choosy Ones, they were probably right, we shouldn't have been eatlng meat. Not any meat. No, siree, I reckon they was right now, in hindsight.

But my pa, he sits in the back, his bulging eyes sunken in his eye sockets like boiled eggs. And he watches them potatoes. And after some hours ma comes out and then pa goes back inside to sleep. Ma sits down yawning, watching them potatoes with the shotgun by her side.

And they do this every night.

And one night I hear pa shouting and I wake up and ma tells me to hush and get back in bed. I see ma take pa's revolver and carry it in her right hand as she heads outside to see what the fuss is.

I creep on down the stairs after her. I'm a little scared, but as I said before, you don't get scared much when the hunger is eating you.

So I'm creeping down the stairs like a skeleton in rags. Pa's outside. I know that, 'cos that's where the potatoes is and that's where I hear the noise coming from. I walk out onto the deck and I see Pa is talking to some zombies. I'm saying they zombies but they ain't really. They're just hungry people look like zombies.

Pa is shouting at 'em.

"Get the fuck off my land!" he says.

I can see he's got the shotgun up by his cheek. It's heavy, I know it is, 'cos we're hungry and everything is heavy when you're hungry. I can also see the shotgun is trembling a little. And it ain't 'cos pa's scared. No, siree, pa ain't scared, but he's tired and hungry.

I see ma is holding up pa's revolver in her hand. Actually she's clutching it with two hands like you'd hold a rope. And the revolver in ma's hand is shaking and this is because ma is scared. I can tell ma is scared 'cos of how she's speaking.

"Get, get," she's saying.

And she only uses one word at a time when she's scared. I seen this before. But I'm watching my pa with the shotgun up by his cheek like a long arm pointing at them zombies. And I know he's thinking he might need to fire a warning shot. But he doesn't want to. The last thing we need is more noise to attract more attention to us.

But it's a hard choice to make. I can tell, 'cos pa is sticking his tongue into one cheek and then into his other cheek. He's biting his lip too. He's trying to figure out what to do.

"Go on, get lost, get the fuck off my property, before I shoot your ass," he says.

And then I looks over at the zombies. There's three of them. It's a family I'm pretty certain. I'm only six, remember, but I'm pretty certain that they's a family.

There's the ma and the pa and the daughter. She's maybe ten years old. I dunno, it's hard for me to say, but I reckon she's ten. She's definitely not old enough to be a woman. She's clutching a couple of potatoes in her dirty little hands. They're filthy hands, 'cos they been digging in our yard, stealing our potatoes.

"Leave the potatoes," says pa.

The little girl, she gets scared now and drops the potatoes. The ma grabs the daughter and turns around. The pa picks up the potatoes the girl dropped and then he turns around to leave. But pa won't have it like that.

"I said drop the fucking potatoes," he says.

Thing is, yeah, it's the Forever Famine, but we ain't gonna miss two potatoes. I mean, we've got a lot of green leaves in this backyard. A lot of potatoes are sleeping under the ground. I'm only six but I can tell.

The light from the kitchen is bleeding out into the yard and it's making big, fast moving shadows of us.

Ma says to pa, "let them have the potatoes." But pa is already right behind the man and he lifts up the butt of the shotgun and he goes to smash it against the man's head.

But pa has not been seeing so good since the Forever Famine started and he just glances the butt off the man's head. I see pa twirl around like a ballerina. He's barely able keep his balance. The man stumbles and grabs at the back of his head, dropping them potatoes he was holding.

He tells his family to run, but these zombies are hungry and they can barely walk faster than a shuffle.

Pa gets a hold of his self and steadies his self.

"That's right, get," he says, "and don't never come back."

Ma is relieved. She looks at me with a frown.

"I told you to get to bed and hush up," she says.

"It's okay," pa says, "let's have some of them potatoes."

And he picks up the two dropped potatoes and a couple others that them zombies had unearthed and ma cooks them for us. Boils them, and I'm full after just one potato. And I sleep so well that night. My belly is warm and I feel full. The coldness leaves me for a few hours and that's good, too. But he comes back later with vengeance.

So, the next night is when I see my pa kill a man. It's the same routine. Ma is out there on her watch and I reckon she must have fallen asleep. She wakes up startled 'cos there's like a dozen folks in our yard, pulling out all the potatoes they can. I hear her shriek. Pa doesn't.

Ma comes running in the house. Well, maybe not running, but moving pretty good considering how hungry we all is. She's yelling.

"Pa!" she yells, "pa, I need help, they's stealing our potatoes."

And then pa wakes up and he grabs the revolver. See, ma has the shotgun 'cos whoever's outside gets the shotgun.

Pa runs downstairs to see what's going on. He's not really running, but you understand how it is. Pa's only wearing his pajama pants. And like the night before, I creep out of my room to see what's going on. This time I'm scared. There's something in ma's voice that gives me dread.

And I creep downstairs and hang by the corner of the kitchen where the door opens out to the yard. There's so many zombies out there. Our yard is full of them.

"Get out of my house!" yells pa, "get the fuck out!"

Pa doesn't really know what to do. He's holding the revolver down by the side of his leg. This time the light by the deck is on but it's not strong. And the shadows make these people, these zombies, look real scary to me. They have like many arms, and shadows and flesh and clothing move like snakes.

Pa puts the gun up in the air like I've seen 'em do it when they's letting sprinters run off. And the crack is so loud that for some seconds after I can't hear nothing.

Then I hears whistling in my ears and then the sound comes back. The zombies freeze for a second and the gun shot split the air and made everyone quiet like.

Then this man turns around and looks at pa. He's not so much a zombie, and I know his kind. Ma and pa and others had told me about folks like him. He's the Black Boots. These are those men they used to call police. But that was when they wasn't the enemy. When they was our friends. But that was a long time ago. Before the Forever Famine.

Now these Black Boots work for them Shark Faces and they alls trying to screw us zombies.

So this Black Boot looks up at pa and he says very menacing like, even though his words is polite. He says, "put down the gun, sir." And he walks up to pa and I can see his teeth shining white and his cheeks pink as apples. He doesn't look like us, his eyes aren't shrunken in his face and his skin ain't gray.

"We're taking what we need for the community," the Black Boot says.

But even at six years old I know he's a liar. I can tell. I can see what they's doing. He's got them zombies picking our potatoes so they can take it to the Shark Faces and the other Black Boots. These zombies helping the Black Boot might get something for their troubles, but not much.

So the Black Boot walks up onto the deck like this is his house and he puts out his hand for pa to put the gun in. I'm hoping pa won't.

"Leave us alone," ma says, her voice quaking. She's scared, I can tell. The Black Boot is mean looking. Zombies don't look mean, but them Black Boots with the pink skin and white teeth, them look menacing. And he looks at ma real mean like and he snatches the shotgun away from her.

I think he's gonna shoot pa, 'cos he points it at my pa's belly. And I get scared, real scared. I feel warm liquid down the side of my leg. Only later do I figure I pissed myself.

And pa looks at ma and out of the corner of his eye I reckon he sees me. His hand is looking like it's gonna give the Black Boot the revolver. But the last minute I sees pa squeeze the trigger.

The sound doesn't seem as loud this time. Maybe 'cos I'm used to it now. But I see the smoke like a gray snake, slither out the gun. And then I sees the Black Boot's face and he's looking all surprised. And then I look down where he's looking and I see this dark red button where he's hand is going to. He clutches at it like he wants to pull the button off.

But he can't see, 'cos the button is wet and growing bigger on his white shirt. Pa shot the man in the chest. And I sees him drop to his knees and then fall forward onto pa's legs. Pa looks down at the man and then steps away. The shotgun falls on top of ma's toes and she's not wearing no slippers. She winces.

The other zombies who had come to help the Black Boot are shuffling and running out of our yard. But they's taken all our potatoes. Almost all our potatoes.

"Shit," says pa, "I reckon I's killed him."

Ma looks at pa and then at the Black Boot lying by pa's feet. She doesn't say nothing.

"I think we's in trouble now," says pa.

Ma shakes her head. She looks at pa carefully like she can't quite make him out. She swallows.

"We could eats him," she says to pa. "Then there'll be no evidence you done nothing."

Pa looks at ma real slow. He's thinking about her idea. I step out onto the deck. Ma can see I pissed myself. She looks at me and then looks at pa again. Pa understands.

"Yeah, we'll eats him," he says.

They drag him inside the house and then out again into the garage. Pa tells me to go with ma into the house. He tells her to get him his knives. When we get back to the garage the Black Boot is naked. He's got nothing on.

"Take him to find some potatoes," pa says to ma.

Ma nods and takes me by the hand. I reckon it's close to sunrise now. Maybe an hour away. Me and ma, we go and look for potatoes. We can only find six. But ma thinks that's good.

"It's enough to make a good stew," she says to me.

And when she smiles I sees her rotten teeths and the gaps where teeths shoulda been.

We go back into the house and ma takes me upstairs to give me a bath. Then she dries me up and tells me to dress.

She goes downstairs to prepare the stew. She's got a big pot. I hear her tell pa that it's 62 quarts. It'll hold a good chunk of that Black Boot.

I come downstairs and can smell the flesh cooking in the pot. It smells like shit, literally and I want to puke. But ma slow cooks it for hours. At around lunchtime that day we start eating the Black Boot. It's hard for me to keep it down. It's hard for ma and pa to keep it down. But the hunger, like I told you, gets you to do things.

And the next day, and the day after that, we keep eating the Black Boot. And I'm starting not to feel hungry very often. I'm starting to remember what it's like to have food in your belly.

And then the worst happens. I did thought that the worst to happen was the Forever Famine. I did thought that nothing could be worse than the Forever Famine.

Being hungry and cold and having death knocking at the door all the time was the worst.

But it wasn't the worst. Not by lots. The worst came the day after I started feeling full.

The Black Boots come looking for my ma and pa and me. We's sleeping sound in bed when I wake up to big sounds like doors breaking and windows smashing. It sounds like a hurricane has hit our house.

I wake up and creep round my bed to the door. I sees the Black Boots storming up our stairs and down the hallway to ma and pa's room. Not long after, they's got ma and pa and they's dragging them downstairs. Ma is yelling and crying and pa is too beat up to try anymore. I see blood is dripping from his nose and he's got a big welt on the side of his cheek.

One of the Black Boots sees me.

"There the little fucker is," he says. And he comes and grabs me by the elbow. I try to escape, I's kicking and punching and biting him. He takes his black stick and he whacks me over the head.

When I wake up I's outside with ma and pa. We's by our backyard fence and our hands and feet are tied.

There's four Black Boots looking at us, and there's two families of zombies looking at us, too. Them zombies is licking their chops. We can't move for our feet is tied.

"Shoot the adults," says the one Black Boot. "I want the boy for myself."

That Black Boot is the one who grabbed me. I remember him. Before I can think of what he really said, I hears two cracks of the whip. Only nobody's got whips. Then I realize they's gone and shot ma and pa. I turn to look and ma and pa is lying down on the ground in lumps next to me.

Ma is facing me and I can see her eyes. They's still open, but they look like marbles. Them don't look real. And I look back at the Black Boot and all I can see is a big smirk on his face, and I want to run up to him and kill him. But I'm only six and my feet is tied. The Black Boot nods at the zombies and they come and carry ma and pa away and I never see 'em again. But I knows what they'll do to 'em. Ma and pa is gonna be eaten.

And the Black Boot takes me and tosses me over his shoulder. "You gonna live with me boy," he says. And he don't sound real friendly. And I's scared again, but I don't dare piss myself 'cos I know he won't like it and he'll give me a whipping. I'm only six years old but I knows what the future has in store for me, and it ain't pretty.

And I was right. That night them beatings started. He brought me home to his family. He had a fat son with a fat face. His son I reckon's maybe ten years old. His wife is fat, too. Thems been eating real good. I can see it on their fat pudgy faces and the flabby rolls bursting out from under their shirts.

"This is what the zombies are like," the Black Boot says to his wife and son. "We're going to make an example of this one. These animals are not going to drive the world to hell."

And I figure something important then. This Black Boot is calling me an animal. And I remember what one of them Choosy Ones said once. I heard 'em say, "a dog is like a pig is like a child is like a man. They're all the same. You treat one badly and you'll soon be treating them all badly."

The Black Boot takes this thick wooden stick from beside the cupboard and I sees him lick his lips. He brings the stick over to where I is, and I can see it real good now. It's thick as my ankle. Not real thick, but thick enough it won't break. And the Black Boot takes to smacking the stick against his palm.

I hears it go "thwack, thwack." And I gets scared. He likes that. Then he takes the stick and he starts to beat me with it. And the last thing I remember is my warm piss trickling down my leg. I pass out.

When I'm awake again, I's in the basement and I's tied to a metal bed with a thin mattress on it. By the side is a can. I figure this is where I piss and shit.

The boy comes down with a plate of something. It's a thin soup. Maybe there's a leaf or something in it. I think I recalls a bit of green in it. He puts it just out of my reach and he watches me swallow and salivate.

The drool leaks out the corner of my lips and drops on the floor. The boy looks at me and starts laughing.

He points at me and he's laughing, throwing his head up towards the ceiling. You think he'd never seen something so funny.

Then he pushes the bowl of food close to me and I reach out for it greedily. Maybe I shoulda been more discreet, but I's hungry. And just as I touch the rim he pulls it away again. And he's laughing like he's never seen something so funny in his whole life. But that's okay, 'cos a big tongue of this soup falls over the side of the bowl and I can just reach it. My arm is way back, tied to the bed and I's almost dislocating my shoulder, but I can reach the broth.

It's on the cement floor and I's taking to licking it up. It gets cold real quick but it still tastes good, so I'm licking it up. You've gotta understand the hunger during the Forever Famine. It makes you do stuff. That's the God's honest truth. You do stuff just to survive.

And I remember thinking as the boy is laughing at me as I's rubbing my tongue raw on the cement floor. I's thinking how they's treating me like an animal 'cos it makes it easier for 'em to beat me that way.

And the boy leaves then, kicking the bowl closer to me. More broth spills out and I lick it up. Then I figure I can reach the bowl so I takes it and drinks it down real quick, in case they change their mind.

This is the Forever Famine, and it goes on like this for eleven more years. Ma and pa is dead and Black Boot beats me regular like. Eleven years they just give me enough food to keep me alive. And I'm living in this filthy basement and I don't dare cry out. No, siree, Black Boot will come quicker than a flash and beat me unconscious.

So I wish I's been a Choosy One. They's all dead by the third year of the Forever Famine. And I wishes I was dead too. But I's six years old, then seven, eight, nine and so on. And I just can't not eat. The hunger won't let me. I's too young and too fragile to starve myself.

So I's living like this, in a hell hole during the Forever Famine. But when I turns twelve or there's about. I can't tell time no more so I don'ts really know how old I is. But I reckon I's about twelve when I start to work on the mattress springs.

And slow, real slow I start to bend 'em and over the months and the years they break off and I hide 'em in the mattress cloth. And I take my time and I twist these pieces of metal together. It takes me a long time, but slowly I see this long spike start to form. And I get real hungry. But this ain't the hunger of the belly. This is the hunger of the mind.

And I feed this hunger with the flames of hatred. I feed it by remembering ma and pa and how the Black Boots just shot 'em dead right in front of six year old me. And I bite my tongue and I take the beatings that come and it feeds the hunger in my mind.

When I'm about sixteen years old, my mind hunger is like a blazing fire. A bonfire of hatred that burns so hot, the belly hunger is no longer cold. And I have this long spike with a handle on the end. I reckon the spike made from the mattress springs is six inches long and it looks like a T. And that T part, the handle fits real comfortable in my palm. Over the years I's shaped it to fit like a glove in my hand. The spike pokes out between my middle fingers.

I caress it and I feel it in my palm. It's my best friend. I play with it all the time when I can. I swing my arm around and watch it glint as it catches the light from the moon. It feels comforting to me, and I knows what I'm gonna do with it. I'm hungry. My mind is aching with starvation.

So when I's about sixteen, I takes a dump right at the end of my rope. But I leave the shit on the floor. I don't use no can they's given me. I knows this'll piss off the Black Boot. That's my plan.

And he comes down one night to make sure I's still healthy enough for beatings and to make fun of me. And he sees the shit and he almost steps in it.

"You fucking little bastard," he says to me. "I'm gonna make you clean that up with your mouth you piece of shit."

But I's no longer scared. I pretend though. I cower way back in the corner of the basement by my bed. I does this 'cos it'll give me more reach from the rope tied to my hand.

And the Black Boot comes up to me and he's got his big stick ready and it's above his head and he's just about to lunge down and whack me with it.

This is when I takes my opportunity. I jumps up at him and my right hand comes swinging for his neck. It's exposed you see, and I can see his vein there. It's like a big snake and I aims for it.

You gotta understand, the hunger makes you do stuff. The Forever Famine was a long time. And my hatred was the only thing fed during the Forever Famine. And I's starving for revenge. And Black Boot, he's not expecting nothing see, 'cos I's never stood up to him. No, siree, I's just been biding my time.

And my hand connects with his throat, and the spike pushes in just like when you's stick a pin in a pillow, and I sees the spike come out the other side of his throat. His face is making weird contortions. His mouth is open and closing like he's trying to say something but he can't.

He drops to his knees and I hears the stick clanging on the floor. He's grabbing at his neck like he's been strangled. I's pulled out my spike by this time and I can reach for the stick. So I picks it up and I looks at him and I want to smash his fucking face to pieces.

And that's what I does. I smashes his face with the stick until all I can see is a red pulpy mess. It reminds me of squashed raspberries that I seen long time ago.

When I's done finished smashing his face, I reach in his pockets 'cos I know he has a knife and I take the knife and cut the rope that's tied me for eleven years. And his wife must've heard something 'cos I hears her at the top of the stairs.

"Clive," she says. "Clive are you down there?"

And I can see her shadow in the door, and I hides just by the side of the stairs where she can't see me. And I hears her coming down, the stairs creaking. She's slow and I's getting impatient. She makes it down to the landing and I sees her holding a gun in front of her and then she sees the Black Boot and she says "Oh, my God."

I dunno why she says that, God's been dead for years, you understand. And that's the God's honest truth.

And she turns around to look for me. And I'm right there behind her and I smash her with the stick.

And now this stick, which has taken lots from me. This stick has beaten me dozens of times, I's now using it for revenge. And I smashes her face, that face that laughed at me for eleven years. I smashes that face until it's a raspberry mess like the Black Boot's.

And I sees myself looking over her and I's panting like a wild dog. Like I remembers what wild dogs might have been like. See, you gots to understand there are no animals anymore. Not where the peoples is living. And I's sweating and shaking. I'm tired as all hell.

And then that fucker comes downstairs. The boy who beat me, too, and laughed at my face. He's now probably twenty or so and he's a big strapping lad. Remember I's small now. 'Cos of the Forever Famine and the hunger. I never did grow too big.

So I grabs the gun and shoots him three times in his chest. One of them misses. And he still comes for me like a fucking zombie. But just as he reaches me he stumbles to his knees and then I takes my time to put his brains all over the place.

I shoots him right through the eye, and his brains like red porridge spray out the back. Yes, siree, I kills those fuckers who done me real wrong. And I ate sorry.

And then I eats 'em. Over the next couple of weeks I eats them. And over the first few days as I get my strength back I realize something terrible's happening. Here in this neighborhood, the place where I's been locked in the basement, this is the place of Black Boots.

And so one night I goes looking at the neighbors house, and in the basement window I peeks in and what does I see but a young girl. Maybe my age, tied to a bed, and I can sees the beatings on her scrawny body. So I breaks into the house real quiet like and I climbs up the stairs to the master bedroom.

And what do you know, two fat fucks, a Black Boot and his fat wife are snoring sound asleep. So I takes my spike and I drive it right through Black Boot's eye. It's like I'm driving spikes on a railroad. And I guess in a way I is, 'cos this is the freedom railroad. And I does the same with her.

They don't have no kids. So I rescue this young girl in the basement and I take her over to my house and we eats our fill. And we've got more meat now too. When my Black Boot is all eaten we eats hers.

And then the twos of us go to the neighbor, and what do we find, another zombie tied in the basement. Not real zombies you understand, just poor kids like us, eaten alive by the Forever Famine. And we goes in and up to the big bedroom. And I've developed a signature now you see. I drive the spike through the Black Boot's eye, and she stabs the woman in the side of the neck with a knife and the blood sprays up against the closet like a guy taking a piss. And some of it is sprays on us and it's warm and tastes like metal.

And now there's three of us zombies. And the Forever Famine is ending and food starts to slowly come around again. No animal meat. No, sirrree. We's just slowly getting back to normal, so it's things like potatoes and veggies. Slowly we gets fruits and grains and stuff like that.

But nobody eats meat no more. The Choosy Ones were right. We's slowly learning to protect the Earth. But my work ain't done. No, siree. We zombies need revenge and we ain't gonna stop 'til all the Black Boots and theys families are dead. Yes, siree. That's the God's honest truth.

And we zombies of the Forever Famine are hundreds. And we're making our killing with Black Boots and we're getting fat on Black Boots. And the authorities are trying to figure it out. Why we so fat, that's what they wants to know. But killing is getting hard. Yes, siree.

I'm fat, and killing the Black Boots is getting harder, and it's killing us too. Us zombies is getting disease and fat and dying. But we won'ts be finished 'til the Black Boots is done in.

And in my city. There's just six Black Boots left and we has thirty seven zombies. So it'll all be over real quick. That's the God's honest truth.

About Jason Blacker

Jason Blacker was born in Cape Town but spent most of his first 18 years in Johannesburg. His thirst for justice and peace for all humanity was formed in the African sun. Currently he lives in Canada.

He writes hard boiled as well as cozy mysteries, action adventure, thrillers and literary fiction under his own name. Jason Blacker also writes poetry and daily haikus at his haiku blog.

You can find his haikus and other poetry at his website www.haiqueue.com.

To stay up to date and learn about new releases be sure to visit www.jasonblacker.com where you can find more information about his writing and upcoming projects.

If you enjoy space opera in the tradition of Star Trek then take a look at Jason Blacker's pen name "Sylynt Storme". It is under the name Sylynt Storme where you can find both sci-fi and vampire fiction written by Jason Blacker.

"Star Sails" is the space opera series and "The Misgivings of the Vampire Lucius Lafayette" is his vampire series.